Reconciliation

SEARCHING FOR AUSTRALIA'S SOUL

NORMAN C. HABEL

HarperCollins*Publishers*

HarperCollins_Publishers_
First published in 1999
by HarperCollins_Publishers_ Pty Limited
ACN 009 913 517
A member of the HarperCollins_Publishers_ (Australia) Pty Limited Group
http://www.harpercollins.com.au

HarperCollins_Publishers_

25 Ryde Road, Pymble, Sydney, NSW 2073, Australia
31 View Road, Glenfield, Auckland 10, New Zealand
77–85 Fulham Palace Road, London, W6 8JB, United Kingdom
Hazelton Lanes, 55 Avenue Road, Suite 2900, Toronto, Ontario M5R 3L2
and 1995 Markham Road, Scarborough, Ontario M1B 5M8, Canada
10 East 53rd Street, New York NY 10022, USA

National Library of Australia Cataloguing-in-Publication data:

Habel, Norman C.
Reconciliation: searching for Australia's soul.

   Includes index.
   ISBN 1 86371 759 5

   1. Reconciliation. 2. Reconciliation - Religious aspects.
   3. Aborigines, Australian. 4. Spiritual life. 5.
   Australia - Race relations. I. Title.

291.440994

Cover: _The Fountain of Tears_ is located on Kaurna land at the site of the former
Colebrook Home in Eden Hills, S.A. and was crafted by Silvio Apponyi, with the
assistance of Kunyi McInerny, Tjula Pole and Sheree Rankine. It was created by the
former residents of Colebrook Home and the Blackwood Reconciliation Group. The six
faces on this sculpture represent Aboriginal families weeping for their stolen children.

Printed in Australia by Griffin Press Pty Ltd, Adelaide on 79 gsm Bulky Paperback

9 8 7 6 5 4 3 2 1   99 00 01 02

Acknowledgements
The author and publisher wish to thank those who have given us permission to reproduce
copyright material in this book. Particular sources of print material are acknowledged in
the text. Every effort has been made to trace the original source material contained in this
book. Where the attempt has been unsuccessful, the publishers would be pleased to hear
from the author/publisher to rectify any omission.

CONTENTS

To
Janice Orrell and Anjali Habel-Orrell
and
to the stolen children
whose story
has brought Australians together

PREFACE

I have written this book as an advocate of reconciliation between the indigenous and non-indigenous peoples of Australia. As I wrote the text, I rehearsed my own history — a journey from an isolated racist rural background to the contemporary political context of the search for reconciliation in Australia. As I explored the vision of reconciliation I came to realise its profound significance for Australia.

Immediately after the 1998 election was decided, the Prime Minister of Australia announced that he would pursue the process of reconciliation with the goal of finalising a document of reconciliation in the year 2001. On the surface, the Prime Minister's goal is laudable. When questioned on television about the government making a formal apology, at least for the injustices perpetrated on the stolen generation, Mr Howard repeated his earlier stance.

The Prime Minister stated that he was personally sorry for what had happened but that there would be no formal apology by the government. He claimed to be the Prime Minister of the present generation and that this generation was 'not responsible' for what had happened to the stolen generation and certainly not for what had happened to the preceding generations.

A public apology is but one part of the reconciliation process in the social domain, but a necessary one. To suggest that those in power today have no responsibility for the injustices caused by the policies of past governments is to repudiate social justice as integral to the political process. The present government has a responsibility to those who have suffered because of the gross injustices to indigenous Australians in previous generations, even if contemporary individuals did not personally commit these injustices.

The process of authentic reconciliation requires that we who are the descendants of the European immigrants to this land no longer hide the shameful parts of our history — the atrocities inflicted on Aboriginal Australians. Reconciliation requires that we seek to understand the indigenous people of our land by valuing their culture, exploring their hidden histories and listening to their stories of resistance and suffering.

A journey of understanding can be painful. It was for me.

It can also be revealing, opening new ways to understand ourselves, our identity as immigrant Australians. This journey not only takes us to the sites where massacres, atrocities and desecration occurred, but also to the spiritual world experienced by the indigenous people of Australia. This journey leads us to explore the soul of Australia, those spiritual dimensions deep within this land that characterise who we are.

People such as David Tacey in *Edge of the Sacred*, Tony Kelly in *A New Imagining* and Veronica Brady in *Caught in the Draught* have sought to explore Australia's soul from various perspectives. My goal is to view the reconciliation process as a search for Australia's collective soul.

My journey has made me realise that authentic reconciliation in the Australian context has a moral and spiritual dimension. I believe this to be true, even if in our so-called secular society Australian political leaders tend to avoid references to God or the spiritual in their public utterances.

I have written this book for the general public, for any who are interested in advocating reconciliation as something more than a political ploy to 'keep the natives happy'. Unlike other books I have written, it is not a theology for the religious elite or a treatise for academics. This book differs also because it reflects much of my own life, my own journey from racist to advocate.

As this book went to press, the Council for Aboriginal Reconciliation released its ten steps to reconciliation, which appeared on the front page of *The Australian* on 5 March 1999. The guarded language of the document reflects the delicate political process involved. While I had hoped the text would have been worded more strongly, several of the statements documented touch on the key issues explored in this book.

Especially significant is the recognition of Aboriginal culture as spiritual, sacred and closely linked to the land. Even more significant is the statement that 'through the land and its peoples, newcomers to this country may taste that spirituality and rejoice in its grandeur'.

This profound hope, together with the stated desire to 'own the truth and heal the wounds' of our past history, to acknowledge that Australia was 'colonised without the consent of the original inhabitants' and to seek 'forgiveness' from the Aboriginal community, point, it seems to me, to an underlying search for more than political peace. Deep within the document there may also lie a search for Australia's soul.

I have many to thank for assisting me in developing this text. I thank the Rainbow Spirit Elders with whom I worked in preparing their text *Rainbow Spirit Theology*. I thank Aboriginal leaders such as Djiniyini Gondarra and George Rosendale, who have been a great source of inspiration.

I appreciate the critical eye of my wife, Jan Orrell, who knows when I fall into select religious rhetoric. I appreciate the expert editorial assistance of Shirley Wurst who enabled me to prepare a final manuscript according to schedule. I thank those who read parts of my work to assess its level and direction — Robert Bos, John Sabel and Peter Pfitzner.

I also thank Basil and Shirley Moore whose experiences in South Africa have sharpened my conscience to injustices.

GLOSSARY

The following glossary is designed to assist the reader to appreciate some of the terms used in this work. I have tried to clarify how I am using these terms without being too technical. Attempting this glossary is rather precarious, however, since many of these terms are quite 'slippery' in common usage and defy simple definition.

Aborigine: a term used for indigenous peoples throughout the world, but in Australia also used as a short form for an Australian Aborigine. The term Aborigine is to be preferred to Aboriginal, which is an adjective not a noun.

Indigenous: some dictionaries define 'indigenous' as 'those born in a country'; in this text I follow the usage of United Nations documents and use the term to refer to pre-colonial peoples originating in or native to a region.

Immigrant Australians: those Australians, born in Australia, whose ancestors immigrated to Australia as part of the colonial process and who are now seeking to come to terms with their colonial heritage; the expression 'European Australians' is too limiting since it focuses on their geographical place of origin rather than on their immigrant status in the land.

Spiritual: that depth dimension in a person, people or place which links with the mysterious, the spirit, a presence, a deity or the 'numinous other' in the world.

Spirituality: the distinctive way a community or individual connects with the spiritual, the spirit or the deity in worship and life in a given location or tradition.

Spirit: the spirit being or spirit force designated the Spirit of God in the Scriptures and the Spirit by some Aboriginal writers.

Holy Spirit: the title used to designate the Spirit of God as experienced by Christians.

Spirit of the Land: the title given to the Spirit in a given land, place or site as experienced by the indigenous people before and after colonisation, and potentially, also by immigrants to the land; the expression 'Spirit of the Land' is used by Galarrwuy Yunupingu and others to describe the creating, life-giving Spirit in the land of Australia (Yunupingu 1996, p. 10); this term is often abbreviated to the Spirit; 'Land' is capitalised to indicate that it is part of a title.

Creator: the creator of the universe in many religious traditions; sometimes called God the Father in the Christian Scriptures and El or YHWH in the Hebrew Scriptures.

Creator Spirit: the designation used by the Rainbow Spirit Elders and others for the creating power known to Christians as the Creator and experienced by indigenous Australians as the Spirit of the Land under various names.

God of the Land: the spiritual force or Spirit in a given land which the people of the land experience in relation to that land and worship as a deity at sacred sites in the land.

Cross: the symbol of the suffering Spirit experienced in Christianity as the God who became incarnate, suffered, was crucified and died in the historical person of Jesus Christ.

Land: 'land' has several meanings depending on the context. 'Land' may refer to Australia; to property owned and worked by immigrant Australians; to that domain or 'mother' from which indigenous Australians believe they originate and which they believe has a deep spiritual dimension.

INTRODUCTION

ON BEING AN ADVOCATE

I believe that Christians can be agents for this process
of reconciliation in the community. However, I believe
they must declare that they stand with the Aboriginal
people in this struggle: they cannot be middle men [*sic*]
...Djiniyini Gondarra (Council 1997a, p. 39)

My search

I am an Australian, a fifth generation immigrant Australian.
For a long time I have wondered what it means for me — for
all of us — to be Australian. I have reflected on our spirit,
our character, our identity as Australian. My ancestors were
German but they settled on land taken from the indigenous
people of Australia. My ancestors left Germany, according to
popular legend, to avoid being drafted into the Prussian
army. Australia was a land of goodwill where they believed
they could live at peace.

My Australian roots reach deep into the land. My great-
grandfather joined the gold rush in Victoria and scraped
together enough money to buy a farm in Western Victoria.
He discovered a piece of black soil — it reminded him of his

1

homeland — and established a small farm near Lake Linlithgow. By then the Aboriginal people of the region had been totally dispossessed; only a remnant survived to work as labourers on local farms.

My great-grandfather taught us all to love the land as our home, to preserve it as a precious gift from God. He even did battle with local farmers who pulled up the young gum trees he had planted around the lake. According to the English locals, the land was for sheep, not for 'pleasure parks'.

As an Australian, the land and the history of this land are part of me, part of my soul. As an Australian, I want to know my identity — my total identity — not a version limited by narrow political, religious or economic interests. As an Australian I am — like many others — still searching for the soul of Australia, that deep spiritual centre which informs our character, the song that 'sings' our identity. Artists, poets, writers and thinkers have pursued this search in one direction or another. From Banjo Paterson to Arthur Boyd and now David Williamson, the search continues. On rare occasions, country folk such as my father would also admit to signs of the sacred simmering in this land:

> The pulsing presence
> erupts but rarely from this land
> before the immigrant
> who when it does
> avoids the glare
> for fear of being lampooned
> in the pub,
> yet with a drink or two
> might say 'Struth
> I felt it there,
> the glare —
> bloody oath I did'.

At the time of the bicentenary, Tony Kelly explored the poets and prophets for 'soul searchings' in the past. To speak of the soul — the song beneath, the spiritual down under — is not something that comes easy for immigrant Australians. We tend to hide our deeper side, to keep our searchings private. Yet, as Kelly says,

> [w]e have located such a search as a legitimate and, indeed, necessary exploration. It is true as we have had plenty of occasion to note, that Australian culture is not particularly hospitable to what we are about. The 'narrowspeak' of our age, perhaps even the ironic reserve we favour, makes it a difficult task. Yet, at a time when Bicentenary Australia is in danger of losing its soul, it is also a good time to try to save that soul as best we can. (Kelly 1990, p. 21)

The current reconciliation process in Australia is, it seems to me, also part of that search. At least it has the potential to be. The process may be downgraded by petty politics, guilt trips, patronising clerics and trivial interests. Yet, there are those who see in the current reconciliation process an opportunity to unite Australians — especially indigenous and non-indigenous Australians — in a just and generous way. In so doing, who we are as Australians may be discovered anew. We may, in the process of reconciliation, discover something more about our deeper self, our soul.

My encounter

Since the bicentenary Australians have been confronted persistently by conflicting forces at work in our society — forces both for and against reconciliation. I am writing because my encounter with those forces has both stirred and stunned me. I am no longer writing for myself but for Australians — or rather with Australians — who share the vision of reconciliation as more than a passing political phase.

My encounter began some years ago, I suppose, when I first met George Rosendale. Even though I had studied

Aboriginal culture and taught Aboriginal religion, it was only when George told me his family story that it all became personal and pressing. My search was no longer understanding what happened in the past when my great-grandfather lived, but how my identity, my past, was linked to the Aboriginal heritage of this land. I had embarked on a new journey to become Australian.

George's story is about how his people were massacred without provocation. The zealous Queensland police, on one of their official 'dispersal' assignments, surrounded the Aboriginal people in their camp. One by one, as men, women and children tried to escape, they were shot like wild animals.

By chance, George's mother — only a little girl at the time — was hidden by her mother under the leaf of a large water lily and escaped being killed. She and George's grandmother both survived that massacre and wandered for some time in the outback before being found. Eventually George's mother was taken to the Hopevale Lutheran mission where George was born many years later.

George, too, survived — in spite of the many indignities and insults he experienced. On one occasion, for example, the Queensland police came again, rounded up the entire mission and carted them off to other locations, where they stayed under guard until after the end of the Second World War. The paranoid Queensland authorities, because of the German heritage of the mission, suspected the Aborigines of being spies for the Japanese.

George eventually became a pastor for his own people in Hopevale. There he came to know the meaning of reconciliation in a context that was both painful and powerful. George and his brother Len still remember with deep hurt what happened to their people. Yet they harbour no hatred. Somehow, as Len said, 'The love of Christ has sort of mellowed us.' Or in George's words, 'I can now forgive the zealous Queensland police. But we dare not forget what happened to our people.'

When people such as George and Len Rosendale speak the word of forgiveness, they act as powerful agents in the process of reconciliation. When their word of forgiveness is spoken, it seems to have a force greater than the perfunctory word of absolution spoken in church. Their word hits home and I feel it. Because of people like George and Len, my spirit is driven to join in the search for reconciliation. Their faith and generosity of spirit have stirred me to be an advocate.

My sense of urgency increased with the release of the report on the stolen generation in 1997. The stories in that report are more than dry records of a misguided government policy. They are penetrating cries from the heart which deserve to be heard. They are cries for reconciliation — not from a distant past, but from my own lifetime. They compel me to ask again who I am as an Australian.

Since the release of that report I have been meeting with high school seniors in private colleges. I have discovered, to my dismay, that many of them do not really want to face the wrongs of our past; many do not even want to know about them. They do not feel any sense of shame or responsibility. They want to sweep the uncomfortable past under the rug as if it were irrelevant and worthless. They find numerous excuses to demand their own individual rights, but deny any sense of communal responsibility. Their catchcry is simply, 'Why say sorry? We did not do it.'

The rhetoric of the One Nation Party also dismays me. Their policy documents deride the precious vision of reconciliation and denounce the search for justice — which ought to be honoured as holy — as an ugly 'industry'. The following excerpt from a speech by the leader of the One Nation Party, given in Federal Parliament on 2 June 1998, illustrates my point.

> For many years the activists of the Aboriginal industry and those who peddle their lies have preyed on the collective conscience of other Australians. We have seen the

distortion and blame-filled confrontation of the so-called
stolen generations, sorry days, sorry books and the list
goes on. We are witnesses to the ongoing PR campaign
aimed not at reconciliation but remuneration.

(Hanson 1998, p. 1)

In the light of these and similar encounters, I must
declare myself an advocate of reconciliation, not to peddle
lies but to explore the truth, not to prey on the collective
conscience but to stir it, not to belittle the reconciliation
process as an industry but to promote it as a search for
justice — and, hopefully, a search for the soul of Australia.

My approach

Much has already been written about reconciliation as part of
the political process in Australia. The Council for Aboriginal
Reconciliation, for example, has produced numerous valuable
booklets and study guides. My aim is to supplement these
texts and interpret the reconciliation process in spiritual terms
that reflect aspects of contemporary Australia's diverse
heritage. My work is intended to stimulate dialogue about the
spiritual dimension of this reconciliation process.
Reconciliation in the deepest sense of the concept, I would
contend, is not only political and social, but also spiritual and
human. Furthermore, the soul of Australia is at stake.

I intend my exploration of this topic to be accessible to a
wide audience, and hope it is not too laden with the usual
'ecclesiastical jargon' that theologians like to employ. I am a
theologian. I am also a poet, an advocate and a writer. I am,
above all, a human being who feels the *Angst* of this situation.

One of the things I have done as an advocate was to
serve as a facilitator for a group of indigenous clergy in
Queensland who called themselves the Rainbow Spirit
Elders. Over a period of two years, working together, we
were able to formulate their *Rainbow Spirit Theology*, a

work that is a distinctive part of the reconciliation process within the church. This book demonstrates to Aboriginal and non-Aboriginal Christians one way in which the basic features of traditional Aboriginal culture can be redeemed and integrated into a genuine indigenous Christian faith. This little book is itself a symbol of reconciliation. A few lines from that book will highlight how as advocates of reconciliation the authors have come to terms with more than political rhetoric; they have sought to overcome spiritual estrangement.

> The Creator Spirit is crying because the land is dispossessed. The land is crying because the people assigned by the Creator Spirit to be its custodians have been torn from the land by force. The people of the land are crying because they are unable to fulfil their responsibilities as custodians of the land.
>
> (*Rainbow Spirit Elders* 1997, p. 45)

My starting point for commencing this study is the reconciliation process as it is unfolding within Australia. Similar processes are developing in other countries: South Africa, Canada, Bosnia. *When Powers Fall*, a recent work by Walter Wink, explores the theme of reconciliation in the healing of nations world wide. My concern is with the specifics of Australian history — society, peoples and life. My aim is to focus on the particular goals of the reconciliation process in relation to the tasks that are part of the Australian struggle. My hope is that I can discern a song behind the struggle: the song in their spirit that Australians rarely sing in public.

There are two important tasks involved in understanding the Australian context. The first is to study, analyse and gather as much relevant information as possible, and to focus on what is pivotal to my search for the spiritual. Like any student, I need to do my homework on this complex subject. The second task is to identify how my own personal experiences of racism, of Aboriginal culture, missions, apologies and indigenous anguish influence my search. I do not speak as a missionary who has sought to bring the Gospel to a particular community. I speak as a person moved by social justice issues since the 1960s, when I first encountered the Black Power movement in America and was scared speechless. The risk of speaking as an advocate of reconciliation in the 1990s may be as great as it was in the 1960s. I am taking the risk, however, because I consider the task of great importance for the future of Australia.

One of my fields of study is the Scriptures, especially the Hebrew Scriptures — or in Christian terms, the Old Testament. This means I tend to read a given situation in the light of biblical precedents. Biblical texts are themselves records of the way ancient people of faith interpreted how the spiritual — the biblical God — was associated with particular events, situations and ideas. The Bible is not a collection of general principles, even though some may deduce principles from certain texts. It is a collection of everyday narratives, letters, poems and laws. This intriguing selection of materials is a record of where the Israelite people saw their God speaking or acting at particular times in human history.

When I explore biblical texts as precedents, I am conscious of the literary, social and political context within which they were used — originally, and over time. While there may not be space in this book to elaborate this background to a given text, any discussion of a biblical text in relation to current reconciliation issues will have first taken this connection into account. When dealing with land, for example, I can refer readers to my more technical study entitled *The Land is Mine*. In other cases, I will, where possible, refer to the appropriate research behind the chosen text for those who may be interested.

Another important feature of my approach is that I speak from within my own life experience and my own social background. I do not pretend to be a detached academic in this book. I provide precedents, stories, reflections from my past, fragments of my faith and signposts from my journey that are clues both to my identity as an advocate of reconciliation and to my understanding of its spiritual dimension. In the final chapter of this book I summarise my identity before and after my search for the soul of Australia. I reveal my change of heart as a result of the process.

After studying numerous religions of the world and tolerating grand intellectual schemes called theologies, I find myself on a fragile planet where the majority of the inhabitants are suffering, starving, and oppressed human beings. I find myself in a land where those people who first brought the message of the cross virtually 'crucified' many of the indigenous peoples of the land. Where is God in such an unjust world? Can I find the spiritual in such a land? Can I, listening to the voices of children from the stolen generation, for example, still discern the cross — the pathos — of indigenous Australia? Is that pathos part of Australia's soul?

This book is neither a practical guide for implementing the reconciliation process in a given community, nor a handbook for confronting the numerous social injustices which indigenous Australians have faced — and still face — in Australian society. This book is an invitation to become an advocate of reconciliation, to discern in this process more than a minimal political exercise forced on the Australian government by international pressure or local activists. This book is designed to explore the significance of the reconciliation process for those of us interested in discovering spiritual dimensions in Australia's identity. This book is a part of my search for Australia's soul.

My plan

In chapter 1 I introduce four facets of reconciliation that deserve to be considered by an advocate: vision, challenge, process and search. In this chapter I focus especially on keeping the *vision* of authentic reconciliation alive as an extended struggle in spite of those who would like a 'quick fix'.

Each of the following chapters are integral to my *search* for Australia's soul as part of the reconciliation process. The second chapter introduces the principles and factors that I consider essential to this process and which I explore in various ways in subsequent chapters. At the beginning of this chapter I discern the presence of these principles in relevant precedents from my own experience and the biblical heritage.

Chapter 3 focuses on the *truth principle* by telling the story of Australia's colonial history, especially from the perspective of the oppressed. Seven stories linked with seven sites are chosen to represent seven grave injustices perpetrated on indigenous Australians. As set out in the Appendix, these seven sites of suffering become symbolic locations for seven *rites of healing*. A significant feature of these rites is that the voices from these stories interact with the voice of the suffering God reflected in the seven words from the cross.

Chapter 4 explores racism as the ideology that moved immigrant Australians to perpetrate these ugly injustices. The *justice principle*, while not discussed in a separate chapter, is recognised as integral to every aspect of the reconciliation process.

Chapter 5 emphasises the *identity principle*, recognising and honouring the distinctive Aboriginal culture that preceded colonial invasion. A significant precedent is provided by Abraham who recognised the Creator God of Canaan, the land to which he immigrated.

Chapter 6 focuses on the land and continues a concern for the *identity principle*. This chapter asks how immigrant Australians like myself can empathise with indigenous Australians in both their links with the land and their loss of the land. Culture and land are essential to Aboriginal identity and must be recognised fully in the process of reconciliation.

The *forgiveness* factor introduced in chapter 2 is discussed in chapter 7 — forgiveness is a crucial process in authentic reconciliation. This process involves a basic change of heart, appropriate public apologies, and relevant rites of healing. Preliminary to this analysis, I distinguish between guilt and shame in the current context. At the end of the chapter I suggest a model for an apology for the seven grave sins committed against the Aboriginal peoples.

In chapter 8 I explore the *suffering factor* and highlight three symbols that point especially to spiritual dimensions of the reconciliation process in Australia. The first symbol is that of the stolen children, whose story of suffering functions to bring indigenous and non-indigenous Australians together. The second symbol is that of the suffering servant from the biblical tradition whose suffering effects healing for the people and possibly finds a contemporary fulfilment in the stolen children — and perhaps in all indigenous people who suffered. The third symbol is the cross, the symbol of the suffering God who is experienced in Christianity as Christ crucified — a symbol that points to the presence of the suffering God among the Aboriginal people.

Finally, chapter 9 seeks to illustrate how, by being an advocate and working through the struggle for reconciliation, my identity as an Australian has changed. I outline the key connections with the indigenous peoples of Australia which I believe non-indigenous Australians must make to identify who we are as Australians, and what characterises our soul in this land.

CHAPTER 1

A VISION FOR AUSTRALIA

... in the end, perhaps together, as Aboriginal and non-Aboriginal, the situation can be reached where this ancient, subtly creative Aboriginal culture exists in friendship alongside non-Aboriginal culture. (Royal Commission into Aboriginal Deaths in Custody, cited in Council 1993a, p. 3)

In this opening chapter I identify four facets of reconciliation which occupy the attention of Australians: reconciliation as a vision, a challenge, a process and a search. I emphasise that as an advocate of reconciliation I am concerned about keeping the vision alive and authentic. The strategies of reconciliation as a social and political process are especially the work of the Council for Aboriginal Reconciliation. My concern for the spiritual dimension of the reconciliation process means that my book will focus on reconciliation as a prophetic challenge and especially on reconciliation as a search for the soul of Australia.

Facets of reconciliation

The decade of the 1960s was the age of Aquarius, the age of dreams and visions. Flower power captured the imagination of a few. Radical students aspired to run the universities. And Martin Luther King had a remarkable dream. Many Americans genuinely believed that a new age was dawning: an age of freedom, an era of equality, a brand new day characterised by the greeting 'peace brother' and 'peace sister'.

My memory of those peace days in America is vivid and painful. There was a naive belief abroad that we could achieve almost anything if we had 'love' as our driving motivation. The song said it all: 'What the world needs now, is love, sweet love.' Liberation was in the air. The bold expectation was freedom for all; love would conquer all. The vision was captivating but fleeting. The ghettos that still haunt the American conscience are evidence that the vision has faded. As a Native American scholar said recently in Adelaide, 'reconciliation is not a vision on the American agenda today'.

Reconciliation *is* on the Australian agenda. What is it all about? What is our vision? What do we hope to achieve? How will it affect us as Australians? There are, I suggest, four facets to reconciliation in Australia, facets that can be seen from diverse perspectives: reconciliation as a vision, as a challenge, as a process and as a search. Recognising these will, I believe, give us our bearings as we investigate the significance of reconciliation more closely.

As a *vision*, reconciliation reflects the hopes of participants about the future, the culmination of this process. As a *challenge*, reconciliation forces non-indigenous Australians to come to terms with the hidden side of our history. As a *process*, reconciliation involves a series of strategies designed to achieve its stated goals. As a *search*, however, reconciliation moves all Australians to look for a deeper significance in this process: a search for meaning, for our identity as Australians.

Reconciliation as vision

Visions play a significant role in our lives. They may be inherent in the symbols, standards or songs that inspire us. They may be dreams that drive people like Martin Luther King or Nelson Mandela. They may be obsessions such as those of Adolf Hitler or Pol Pot. They may be the hidden hopes of a deprived people. They rise and fall with the spirit—or spirituality—of the times. Where a vision is caught by a people, however, it can have profound implications for the future of a nation. Without a vision, I suggest, proposed strategies and processes will lack motivation.

The vision of the Council for Aboriginal Reconciliation has its own distinctive focus on land, heritage and justice. That vision, as articulated by the council, is a 'united Australia which respects this land of ours, values the Aboriginal and Torres Strait Islander heritage, and provides justice and equity for all' (Council 1994a, p. 17).

This vision is interpreted from many different angles by the parties involved. Pat Dodson, former chairperson of the council, recognises that reconciliation may mean many things ranging from a handshake with an Aboriginal neighbour to better relations between indigenous communities and other Australians. But, above all, he claims, it 'must mean some form of agreement that deals with the legacies of our history, provides justice for all and takes us forward as a nation' (Dodson 1996, p. 6).

For Dodson and the council, the vision incorporates the hope of a specific document — hopefully by the year 2001 — that will officially recognise the history, rights and culture of indigenous Australians. This vision, however, is far more than a historic document. This vision summons all Australians to identify who we are in relation to the indigenous heritage of our common land. This vision confronts us with our future as Australians.

This vision reminds me of the hopes of the biblical

prophets who dreamed of a day when all peoples would unite in worshipping God, beating their swords into ploughshares and never again learning the art of war (Isaiah 2:1–4). The ideals embodied in this vision are precisely those that many of the biblical prophets proclaimed: justice, respect for land, peace. They are likewise the ideals of other indigenous peoples throughout the world.

For me, as an advocate of the 1990s, these ideals are not pious piffle or political rhetoric. Nor should the text of the council's vision be read in terms of traditional Western ways of thinking. The ideals of this vision call all Australians, as the prophets once did in ancient Israel, to consider what it means to be 'united' as Australians with a history of alienation and exclusion. They invite me — and other advocates — to rethink what we understand by 'respect for the land', a land invaded and settled by European colonists with scant respect for the land. They ask us as immigrant Australians to value a heritage we once derided as 'the work of the devil'. They expect a day when justice and equity will be the provenance of all, especially of those who have been deprived of justice for so long.

Is this vision an impossible dream? It certainly demands a radical reorientation by most non-indigenous Australians. It also challenges indigenous Australians whose lives have been transformed by European culture. It summons us all to ask whether we are serious about the future of Australia as a people who embrace their indigenous heritage. It stands before us as a potential achievement of which we could be justly proud. As the final recommendation of the *National Report* of the Royal Commission into Aboriginal Deaths in Custody states,

> in the end, perhaps together, Aboriginal and non-Aboriginal, the situation can be reached where this ancient, subtly creative Aboriginal culture exists in friendship alongside non-Aboriginal culture. Such an

achievement would be a matter of pride, not only
for all Australians but for all humankind. (Council
1993a, p. 3)

Reconciliation as process

The strategies outlined by the Council for Aboriginal
Reconciliation for achieving reconciliation would suggest
that this vision is not a vague utopian dream nor an abstract
political ideology. These strategies are designed to achieve
one specific goal by the year 2001, namely, 'to prepare the
nation to own the Council's vision' (Council 1994a, p. 17).

To achieve this goal, eight key issues have been identified
as crucial to the educational task in the process of
reconciliation.

Understanding Country: The importance of land and sea in
the Aboriginal and Torres Strait Islander societies.

Improving Relationships: Better relationships between
indigenous Australians and the wider community.

Valuing Cultures: Recognising indigenous cultures as a
valued part of our Australian heritage.

Sharing Histories: A sense for all Australians of a shared
ownership of their history.

Addressing Disadvantage: A greater awareness of the causes
of indigenous Australians' disadvantage.

Responding to Custody Levels: A greater community
response to addressing the underlying causes of the high
levels of Aboriginal and Torres Strait Islander peoples'
deaths in custody.

Agreeing on a Document: Will the process of reconciliation be
advanced by a document or documents of reconciliation?

Controlling Destinies: Greater opportunities for indigenous
Australians to control their destinies. (Council 1994a,
pp. 17–18)

It is significant that this process has been developed in cooperation with the indigenous peoples in the council and owned by many indigenous Australians as an expression of their hope. The cry for reconciliation has risen from the oppressed, the stolen, the dispossessed, the disadvantaged. Their vision of reconciliation confronts us as non-Aboriginal Australians with our past, the dreams of our ancestors, the visions of our missions. Reconciliation is also about owning the past — the wrongs and injustices as well as the visions and dreams — and healing the memories. It is intended to be a process of healing, a process which may take time, but one which is vital to the health of the Australian community.

Has Australia caught the vision? Many organisations, grassroots movements and church bodies are participating in the process. Schools and educational bodies are involved to varying degrees. Something of the groundswell of interest became apparent to me in Adelaide in 1997, when the controversial Pauline Hanson came to town. Instead of focusing attention on the specific location in town where she was speaking, locals decided to march down King William St, the main street of Adelaide, to support multiculturalism in Australia. A few hundred gathered for the Hanson meeting; the crowd who took part in the march was estimated at around 10,000. Among the marchers the spirit of goodwill was remarkable. A sense of solidarity against racism and for reconciliation was evident among all who participated.

On 31 May 1998, a remarkable stone monument entitled 'Fountain of Tears' was dedicated on the site of the former Colebrook Home in Adelaide, where indigenous children from the 'stolen generation' were institutionalised until 1971. That monument not only symbolises the spirit of the reconciliation process and our communal expression of sorrow over what happened to the stolen generation, but also illustrates the force of community action groups supporting reconciliation. The reconciliation process has begun.

Reconciliation as challenge

Reconciliation is an enormous task against seemingly overwhelming odds. The Aboriginal peoples of Australia represent a small minority, which, as far as the Australian authorities are concerned, did not legally exist until 1967. For a long time the indigenous peoples were expected to assimilate or become extinct. For a long time they were dismissed as irrelevant to Australia's future. For a long time they were simply 'the Aboriginal problem'. Now they are the ones challenging non-Aboriginal people with a vision for all of Australians. Now they are the prophetic voices in the land!

The prophetic voice in the reconciliation process confronts some of us — those whose ancestors immigrated to Australia — with our history, our identity. Like a biblical prophet of old, this voice calls us to face the whole story of what happened, the reality of our heritage. We have two hundred years of history that, until recently, has been written from the perspective of the powerful, self-righteous rulers who hid the ugly past. We are challenged now to hear the Aboriginal side of the story and to expose the lies of our history books as a necessary step in clearing the way for reconciliation.

The challenge is also directed at those institutions which preserve Australian memories and relive them in story, art and ritual. It is through these institutions that the past actions of immigrant Australians can become part of who we are. Every year many Australians relive Anzac Day. Every year many also relive Australia Day. On Sorry Day 1998 some Australians remembered the stolen generation. That day was but a beginning of a long process of remembering. Now all Australians are challenged to be part of this process of remembering the hidden stories of the past so that there can be genuine healing in the land.

The challenge, I believe, is especially directed to the churches. The churches were involved not only in bringing the spiritual message of the Gospel to indigenous Australians, but were also instruments of the government — albeit not always willingly — in the administration of unjust government policies. Uncomfortable as the idea may be, I am forced to acknowledge that the institutional churches usually represented the European invaders — not the indigenous inhabitants. The churches belonged to the oppressive majority and promoted Western culture — in spite of the many constructive things they may have done to rescue threatened Aboriginal communities. The churches, therefore, are challenged to play an increasing role in the reconciliation process — perhaps even to act as mediators.

If the churches claim to know the reconciliation process in their worship practices — repentance, confession, forgiveness and healing — then they are challenged to participate in the reconciliation process as part of life, Australian life. They are challenged to come out of their mighty ecclesiastical fortresses and join the struggle for reconciliation as committed people who claim to live as well as preach reconciliation. As Andrew Hamilton claims,

> the gift which the church can offer is nowhere clearer than in the theory and practice of reconciliation. In the first place, the church has recognised the symbols of reconciliation and has developed them ... While these symbols may be rusty in the contemporary church, they are a rich resource for reflection on a symbolically impoverished national life. (1998, p. 51)

Reconciliation as search

The more I research the vision and the challenge of reconciliation both in Australia and in strife-torn countries abroad, the more I realise that reconciliation is an opportunity to explore dimensions beyond the surface politics of our secular society. There is, it seems to me, a search taking place, whether conscious or not, to discern the sacred in our land, to discover our soul as Australians, to probe the spiritual in the process. By undertaking to identify the signals of that search, I hope to analyse the reconciliation process afresh from a spiritual perspective.

A clear signal of that search was evident in the words of David Costello, a young indigenous elder from Hopevale. During a video interview in 1997, he identified the reconciliation process as a spiritual problem.

> We talk about problems, we talk about healing, we talk about reconciliation. But it goes much deeper.
> Aboriginal to Aboriginal, Aboriginal to Australians, Australians to us, Aboriginals to the land. It's a deeper problem. It's a spiritual problem.

There are two dimensions to this search. The first is to discover the soul of Australia as it emerges from this process. The second is to discover where the spiritual, whether immanent or transcendent, is involved in reconciliation within Australia. The searches are related, but deserve to be treated separately. The one may appeal to those who are spiritual but not necessarily religious; the other may make connections for those who still celebrate the mystery of the cross.

The search to glimpse facets of the Australian soul is really a search to discover the deep identity we will all share as reconciled Australians. If immigrant Australians are serious about listening to the story of what happened in the past, learning to value indigenous cultures, finding ways to respect the land as sacred, and participating in rituals of healing, we will begin to change. To be Australian will no longer mean being connected only to convicts, battlers, drovers, explorers, farmers and the like. It will also mean being connected to an indigenous heritage and a history of shame. Making that connection will affect the Australian psyche — if the connection is made with the heart as well as the intellect. Without a change of heart, reconciliation will be a farce.

There are those who would berate me for searching for the spiritual in the Australian reconciliation process. They want to keep the domains of church and state separate, as if God had nothing to do with the latter. They would distinguish sharply between reconciliation as a spiritual process whereby Christians are 'reconciled to God' through the cross of Jesus Christ, and the secular political process whereby two parties in society learn to respect each other and live at peace.

This division, I believe, is simplistic and ignores the fact that such a neat formulation separating these 'two ways' in which God works is a human doctrinal formulation. I see God's gracious presence and power permeating all realms. The history of the Israelites is a story of God's involvement in their total life — social, political and spiritual. The story of Jesus in the Christian Scriptures is as much about liberating the socially oppressed as it is about forgiving spiritual sins. For me, therefore, the search to discern the spiritual in the secular process of reconciliation is not folly or heresy, but a genuine desire to discover the sacred in more than religious contexts.

True and false reconciliation

Walter Wink has made a valuable contribution to an understanding of the reconciliation process by identifying the characteristics of true and false reconciliation. During and after conflicts, those in power often wish to achieve peace at all costs; the result is false reconciliation. The powerbrokers may push for reconciliation between those in power and those rising up against that power. The outcome may be a truce that leaves the weaker group in a worse situation than before — with no redress for the injustices being perpetrated. As Wink illustrates,

> the problem was always presented not as a case of
> injustice but rather as a case of broken human relations
> or a breakdown of communications. The job to be

> done was to *mend the relationship*, not to undo the
> injustice. Invariably the 'little' man [*sic*] was clapped on
> the back, cajoled, reassured, and led to shake hands
> with his oppressor, although no reversal of the injustice
> had taken place. (Wink 1998, p. 25)

Tragically, churches have often fallen into the trap of preaching reconciliation in a variety of contexts without actually committing themselves to struggling on the side of the oppressed and striving for justice for all. Church leaders may call for peace and order in a revolutionary situation only to find they are upholding a corrupt administration based on violence and oppression. Citing Romans 13:1–7 as its justification, the church may actually be condemning the destitute poor to suffer at the hands of the ruling rich. To be neutral in such conflicts is to support the status quo and ultimately the oppressor.

> This false reconciliation was articulated by a South
> African church officer, who maintained that the duty of
> the churches is to be agents of reconciliation. That means
> we must avoid taking sides and be neutral. (Wink 1998,
> p. 26).

Another form of false reconciliation arises when so-called sympathisers hijack the process with instant remedies. They may ask forgiveness, or extend an apology without first listening to the pain, understanding the hidden stories, repenting of the wrong or seeking ways to right the wrong. Wink cites one such case in South Africa where a white theologian addressed a multicultural gathering and asked forgiveness for his role in creating apartheid. His bid for cheap grace was exposed for what it was.

> Another said, 'I don't want nice apologies so white
> people can feel good. What I want is for whites to join
> us in the struggle to dismantle apartheid and create
> justice.' Reconciliation is a process, and the theologian

was aborting that process by leaping over stages of
anger and remorse and the need for acts of restitution.
(Wink 1998, p. 28)

False reconciliation is also promoted when the governing
authorities focus on the superficial dimensions of an issue
within the reconciliation process. Their goal is to process the
matter as quickly as possible within the limited confines of
the political or legal practice, but without taking into
account deeper dimensions that affect the minority group
involved. In the current Native Title debate in Australia, for
example, both major political parties seem to have reduced
the issue to a matter of land management. Many politicians
do not — or will not — hear the voice of the indigenous
people claiming that land is also a deeply spiritual and
cultural reality that affects their very soul, their inner
identity. The Howard government's action of excluding
indigenous representatives from the process of legislating
amendments to the Wik case in 1998 negated the very spirit
of reconciliation.

False reconciliation is just as likely in Australia if the
process is viewed as strictly political, and the deeper cultural
and spiritual dimensions — dimensions that relate to
Australia's very identity — are ignored. Indigenous and non-
indigenous Australians will not be reconciled if we do not
understand each other as more than political players in a
national management game. We will be one only if we
relentlessly pursue the stages and principles of an authentic
reconciliation process.

How far have we come? What steps must still be taken if
we are to achieve authentic reconciliation? Clearly it is an
extended process. A reconciliation document in the year 2001
may be a landmark, but it will only be a stage in an ongoing
process for all the peoples of Australia. Nor is it possible to
articulate a definitive series of steps that, if followed, will
guarantee success. It is probably more important to consider

the governing principles of the reconciliation process within the vision, tasks and strategies identified by the Council for Aboriginal Reconciliation.

These principles will be outlined in the next chapter and their presence in a number of biblical precedents will be identified. The principles include the truth principle, the justice principle and the identity principle. Two additional factors are also involved, namely the forgiveness factor and the suffering dimension. When these principles and factors are taken seriously and not glossed over as a waste of time, true reconciliation can happen and Australia's vision of unity can be more than a dream.

Keeping the vision alive

We are also faced with the task of keeping the vision alive in the face of numerous national distractions including economic growth, the year 2000 Olympics and the self-interested right-wing ideology of the One Nation Party. We are faced with sceptics from both the indigenous and the non-indigenous camps. How do we answer the cry of Kevin Gilbert as recorded by Mudrooroo?

> We have to look at the word 'reconciliation'. What are we reconciling ourselves to? To a holocaust, to massacre, to the removal of us from the land, from the taking of our land? The reconciliation process can achieve nothing because it does not at the end of the day promise justice. It does not promise a Treaty and it does not promise reparation for the taking away of our lives, our lands, and our economic and political base. Unless it can return to us these very vital things, unless it can return to us an economic, political and viable land base, what have we? A handshake? A symbolic dance? An exchange of leaves and feathers or something like that? (Mudrooroo 1995, p. 228)

One purpose of this book is to keep the vision alive by exploring the potential and significance of the reconciliation process for Australians. Another way of stimulating the process of reconciliation is to return to those biblical prophets who have so often, over the centuries, been sources of hope. Their visions of a reconciled world where justice and peace would dwell side by side, like the lion and the lamb (Isaiah 11:2–9), have been an inspiration to many peoples.

The prophet I have always found the most believable is Jeremiah, not because his visions are any less bold in the face of apparently impossible odds, but because he allows us to experience the pain of his personal life with God, with his people, and with the land. It is especially his bond with the land that allows Jeremiah to speak to our situation. For Jeremiah not only sees the land desecrated to the point of devastation, he also hears the land crying, moaning because of the crimes of his people. A symbiotic relationship exists between Jeremiah, God, and the land (Habel 1992). Jeremiah's visions are a sign of hope for those of us who dare to believe that the God who suffered with Jeremiah is the God who suffered on the cross, and is suffering with indigenous people in their struggle for reconciliation today. Jeremiah sees a day when God will be forced to remove the people into exile and reduce the land to *terra nullius*. He sees the land returning to desolation, to the emptiness of a pre-creation state (Jeremiah 4:23–26). He sees doom as inevitable. Yet beyond the doom and the desolation he sees a new day, a day when weeping will cease.

In the imagery of Jeremiah, Israel and Judah are portrayed as two sisters, the two communities that constitute God's people (Jeremiah 3:6–11). Both must suffer exile for their sins and both will be reunited in the land one day. In the midst of her anguish, God hears Rachel weeping for her children. Rachel is the ancestral mother, the symbol of the ancestors of these sisters and indeed of the land itself. As the mother of Israel she continues to cry for her homeless

children. Yet the prophet sees a day when both peoples will
be reconciled and be planted together on the same land.
Jeremiah's vision may help keep ours alive (Jeremiah
31:27–28).

Were Jeremiah listening to the voice of his God today, his
vision of the two sisters may be different, but no less a vision
of God's promise, of sharing, of joining in covenant with
God and each other — in spite of the past. Were Jeremiah
listening to the crying, to the land, to the stories of the
indigenous people among us, I believe he would find hope, a
new planting in this land. Were Jeremiah here today, I hope
the following poem would reflect his mood.

> In the evening when blood smears the sky,
> I saw two sisters talking together,
> the younger heavy with history,
> the older with wisdom.
>
> I saw the trails of these two sisters
> walking gently through the land,
> listening to the cries of the land,
> the secrets of the land,
> the pain of the land,
> listening to the ancient Spirit
> breathing below,
> heavy.
>
> I saw those same sisters weeping together,
> weeping loudly in the night
> for children stolen by policies,
> children stolen by nooses,
> children stolen by promises.
>
> I even saw these sisters
> covering the crying blood,
> looking for an equal place in the sun,
> yearning each to own her own land
> in their common country again.

In the dawn when the blood was covered
I saw these two sisters sit together
under the Southern Cross,
sit in the sand and draw,
sit in the sand and sing,
sing the future together.

CHAPTER 2

PRECEDENTS AND PRINCIPLES

So when you are offering your gift at the altar, if you remember that your brother or sister has something against you, leave your gift before the altar and go; first be reconciled to your brother or sister and then come and offer your gift. (Matthew 5:23–24)

This chapter introduces those principles and factors which I consider crucial to my advocacy of authentic reconciliation, especially the spiritual dimensions. I outline the key features of the truth, justice and identity principles, and the forgiveness and suffering factors. As background to these principles and factors, I discuss briefly several relevant precedents from my own life and from the Hebrew and Christian Scriptures.

Precedents — personal

My brother and I would often fight when we were children. When the fight was over my parents first tried to ascertain what 'really' happened. Then they expected us to 'make up'. 'Shake hands and say sorry!' That was the standard procedure. There was no favouritism, no grudges, no revenge. We each had the same number of garden peas on our plate, the same number of chores to do, and faced the same verdict when we did wrong. There was always forgiveness, and there was always tomorrow as reconciled brothers. In that context we knew who we were and where we stood.

I also remember, in school, studying 'The Fire at Ross's Farm', a poem by Henry Lawson (Knight 1956, pp. 154–7) that struck chords with me. Conflicts between farmers in the rural community could be bitter and prolonged. It often took a disaster to unite the local community again, especially if the problem was between small farmers and 'big' station owners. Bushfires were probably the most ominous disasters we faced every summer. The suffering and disaster that bring both parties together in Lawson's poem are not the deaths of the lovers, as in Shakespeare's *Romeo and Juliet*, but a bushfire that threatened to destroy Ross's farm on Christmas Eve. Ironically my own weatherboard home on our farm in Victoria was burnt to the ground one Christmas Eve — so I always felt for farmer Ross. I felt, too, the joy of reconciliation when the squatter finally condescends to join Ross in saving his crops — and wins back his son in the process. The poem closes with a simple rite — one I remember well from fighting fires — accompanied by a cold beer when the battle against the real enemy was won.

> And when before the gallant band
> The beaten flames gave way,
> Two grimy hands in friendship joined —
> And it was Christmas Day.
> (Knight 1956, p. 157)

Reflecting on these simple precedents from my youth, I can see a number of the principles of reconciliation at work.

By reflecting more deeply on a number of biblical precedents, these principles become clearer. My aim in identifying these principles is to highlight the moral and the spiritual dimensions in the reconciliation process.

Precedents — Hebrew Scriptures

Early in the Joseph story cycle in the Hebrew Scriptures, Joseph is sold by his jealous brothers to a band of passing Ishmaelites. Joseph is 'stolen' to Egypt by mutual consent of all parties — except Joseph, his youngest brother Benjamin, and the absent older brother Reuben. In Egypt the tables are turned and, after a series of manipulated meetings, the day comes when Joseph reveals his hidden identity and publicly weeps on his youngest brother Benjamin's neck. The great lie, symbolised by the blood spattered coat of many colours, is exposed and Jacob, the father, suffers the shame of what his family has done. Subsequently Joseph brings his father to Egypt and provides his whole family with land of their own. Final reconciliation is not achieved, however, until the father dies. At that point the brothers fear, perhaps understandably, that Joseph still bears a grudge and may finally pay them back. To save their necks, they plan a rather devious way to ask forgiveness.

> So they approached Joseph saying, 'Your father gave
> this instruction before he died. "Say to Joseph, I beg
> you, forgive the crime of your brothers and the wrong
> they did in harming you." Now therefore please forgive
> the crime of the servants of the God of your father.'
> (Genesis 50:16–17)

In spite of this rather underhanded request for forgiveness, Joseph willingly accedes and forgives his brothers. Joseph's generosity of spirit is far greater than their grudging request for forgiveness. Joseph's response is genuine tears of reconciliation. The brothers also weep and pledge their obedience to Joseph as loyal servants. The culmination of this encounter is the speech of reassurance which Joseph extends to his brothers. In Joseph's words, the audience hears a faith interpretation of the whole Joseph saga. Joseph, the one who has been wronged and excluded, is now the one who forgives, reassures and restores relations. Joseph mediates reconciliation.

> Do not be afraid! Am I in the place of God? Even though you intended to harm me, God intended it for good, in order to preserve a numerous people, as he is doing today. So have no fear; I myself will provide for you and your little ones. (Genesis 50:20)

In the Joseph narrative, several key features of the reconciliation process are evident. The first is the truth principle. The brothers acknowledge — even if grudgingly — their past 'crime' and the harm resulting from this crime. They even suggest that their father told them what to say, thereby giving their confession added weight. Without acknowledging what had happened in the past and asking forgiveness, the destructive force behind the alienation would continue to fester and the fear of reprisal would intensify. Crucial to this reconciliation was the task of confessing the crime that separated Joseph from the rest of his family and admitting to the lies told to Jacob about his son's 'death'. The truth principle involves the aggrieved telling the story of what happened as they see it, and those responsible acknowledging their part in the story.

The second important component reflected in this text is the forgiveness factor — both seeking and granting forgiveness. This factor involves the party — or parties — in the wrong saying sorry, making public apology or asking forgiveness for past wrongs, even if those wrongs were committed in the distant past. The injured party subsequently extends forgiveness, or gives a public assurance that no grudges or ill will persist against the wrongdoer. The weeping of Joseph and his brothers is an obvious symbol of sorrow and forgiveness. The act of forgiveness, in turn, clears the way for healing, restoration and a new beginning together. The forgiveness factor is not to be confined to the religious domain, but can operate forcefully in the social and political domain. Joseph is more than a brother; he is also a political ruler representing Egypt.

A third feature of this story is the way Joseph interprets the pathos of the past, the history of 'harm' between the two parties. The course of events is not simply accepted as commonplace, but viewed from the perspective of faith. In the agony of the everyday, Joseph discerns a spiritual dimension: 'God intended it for good.' The interpretation of the suffering factor will also be significant as we listen to the stories of the indigenous peoples who suffered and died in this land.

Another pertinent story which is not usually associated with the theme of reconciliation is found in the closing chapter of the book of Job where God pronounces a verdict on Job's friends. 'They have not spoken the truth about me as my servant Job did' (Job 42:7). Job's passionate and cutting speeches were truth — not arrogance, or delusion, or poor theology. By pursuing truth as he experienced it rather than succumbing to the pressures of the pious, Job exposed not only the game God was playing, but the depth of the alienation caused by the ideology of the friends. Their assumption was that a crushed, humiliated and oppressed human being such as Job must necessarily be guilty of some crime or sin. They viewed Job as a sinner, and therefore under God's curse. God endorses the truth principle: the validity of Job's story about how he suffered at the hands of God.

God's way of resolving the alienation that remained at the end of the dialogue is to provide a healing ritual. As an integral part of that ritual, Job intercedes on their behalf. Healing is effected by all parties identifying with a sacrifice, a traditional way of expiating sins and righting wrongs in the

Hebrew Scriptures. By this action, the shame is removed. In this ritual, Job, the party who suffered both at the hands of God and the friends, becomes the facilitator of healing and forgiveness for the friends.

Precedents — Christian Scriptures

The Christian Scriptures also refer to reconciliation between individuals (Acts 7:26; 1 Corinthians 7:11). Within the context of communal worship, Jesus speaks of a situation where two parties need to be reconciled before coming into God's presence (Matthew 5:23, 24). The worshipper must first forgive — or seek forgiveness — in any broken relationship before receiving God's forgiveness. Conflicts between estranged parties need to be resolved before one assumes a posture of peace with God. The forgiveness factor, then, is not confined to relations with God. This factor is integral to the social and political life of those who dare to stand before God and pray, 'forgive us our sins as we forgive those who sin against us'.

Perhaps the most important precedent in this context is a central story of reconciliation in the early Christian community. This community included two main groups: Gentile Christians and a Jewish Christian faction. This faction insisted that it was necessary for Gentiles to be circumcised and keep the law of Moses to become genuine Christians (Acts 15:5). According to the Book of Acts, there was a showdown between the leaders of these two parties in Jerusalem where the inclusive policy of Paul won the day. Paul insisted that the Gentiles did not need to adopt Jewish culture to become Christians. As Christians they could maintain their Greek and Roman identity.

For genuine reconciliation to be possible, according to Paul, the ideology of the law had to be recognised as a divisive force creating alienation between Jewish and Gentile Christians. God, said Paul, has reconciled both parties by removing the hostility caused by the law. God did this, not by divine decree but by divine suffering. The suffering of God in Christ brings both parties together (Ephesians 2:14–16).

Principles

In the light of these precedents, and the wide social context of reconciliation, I believe it is possible to set out a number of key principles and factors which ought be taken into account if reconciliation in Australia is to reach beyond political convenience and into the Australian conscience.

The truth principle

The truth principle states that no serious reconciliation is possible until the suppressed stories are told in public, especially by the oppressed party, and the underlying source of the alienation is exposed. The model of Job 'speaking the truth' from his perspective as an oppressed human — even against God — underscores the significance and spirituality of this principle.

The search for truth in the reconciliation process is more than checking the 'factual truth' which has been uncovered and verified by what Foucault calls 'the regime of truth' established by the dominant party (Foucault 1980, p. 70). The 'truth' of Australian history includes the deep memories of all Australian people, including indigenous Australians, even if those memories do not correspond to archival documentation, and even if they make some of us feel uncomfortable. The story of how a group of Aboriginal people were herded by farmers to the edge of a cliff at Elliston, South Australia, and forced over the cliff onto the rocks below has not been verified by white historians. For Aboriginal people in that country, the story is painfully true and the denial of this truth intensifies the barrier to reconciliation. The voice of the boy who survived that massacre long ago still echoes through the community.

The task of seeking the truth is not simple or singular. In the Australian context three major approaches seem to be operating. The first is to pursue a form of inquiry such as the Royal Commission into Aboriginal Deaths in Custody and the National Inquiry into the Separation of Aboriginal and Torres Strait Islander Children from Their Families. These inquiries demonstrated an open and honest hearing of the stories of the young people involved and raised the consciousness of the wider Australian community to the significance of these stories. The stories, as distinct from the rhetoric of politicians, rang true.

In the South African context, the commission involved is specifically designated a Commission on Truth and Reconciliation. In that context, some people recognised that the truth principle was crucial and that it was perhaps more powerful and positive than the principle of justice. One of the women who addressed the commission expressed her understanding of truth as a healing force in the following way.

> If this commission is only to find the truth so that
> justice can be done in the form of amnesty, trials and
> compensation, then it has actually chosen not for truth
> but for justice. If it sees truth as the widest possible
> compilation of people's perceptions, stories, myths and
> experiences, then it has chosen the road of healing, of
> restoring memory and humanity. (Villa-Vincencio
> 1997, p. 35)

A second approach is to research our history and read the past with a new set of eyes — eyes in search of the suppressed stories of what happened between immigrant and indigenous Australians. The historian Henry Reynolds is a courageous example of this approach, confronting the reader with the documentary evidence of immigrant Australian attitudes and actions towards Aboriginal Australians from the day of Governor Phillip's landing at Sydney Cove. Henry

Reynolds seeks to assume responsibility for reversing what the anthropologist W.E.H. Stanner dubbed 'the great Australian silence'.

A third approach is to hear the stories of Aboriginal people about the local history of their communities. This may be on a professional level: anthropologists such as Deborah Bird Rose hear and record the *Hidden Histories* of the Northern Territory (Rose 1991), or locally: school and community groups listen to members of the Aboriginal community tell their own history — the truth as they experienced it.

The conditions under which people are willing to tell their truth will differ. It depends on whether they are recounting recent wrongs, or researching evils in the more distant past. Churches, community support groups and local advocates can help to create an atmosphere facilitating this process when government authorities are too timid or insecure to expose the lies reflected in the dominant view of history. The dramatic amnesty granted by the government of South Africa facilitated multifaceted truth-telling on a large scale. In Australia, the Council for Aboriginal Reconciliation has provided the official impetus for this process. This council needs continuing support from religious and community advocates to achieve its vision.

Applying the truth principle in the reconciliation process would appear, therefore, to require that

a stories of past suffering, pain and injustice between the alienated parties, from both sides of the conflict, are not suppressed but told over and over again until they become common knowledge in the community;

b truth-telling is endorsed and encouraged by the governing authorities; if they are too weak, the church or some other group with a conscience must take the lead and facilitate telling the story of past relationships;

c past injustices and wrongs are acknowledged by the whole community as part of its common heritage and joint history; and d   the underlying attitudes and ideologies which gave rise to these injustices, and the history of alienation, are recognised and repudiated.

The justice principle

The justice principle requires that past injustices, losses and evils inflicted on the weaker party are addressed by a mutually agreed procedure. By some means, the wrongs of the past must not only be acknowledged but also righted. Injustices of the past must be compensated in some way; restoration ought to be made for past losses. Given the course of history, it is usually not possible to return to the *status quo ante* — the way things were when relationships between the parties began or were peaceful. Nevertheless, a process of restoring the rights, status and honour of the wronged party is necessary if true reconciliation is to take place — even if that process takes some time and is expensive.

Black theologians such as James Cone are extremely forceful in their insistence on justice as a prerequisite for reconciliation. They assert that reconciliation is not possible unless there is a genuine willingness to change the balance of power between the conflicting parties. As Cone says, when

> black people emphasise their right to defend themselves against those who seek to destroy the black community, it never fails that so-called white Christians then ask, 'What about the biblical doctrine of reconciliation?' 'What about Christian forgiveness?' 'Can't black people find it in their hearts to forgive us?' White people who ask these questions should not be surprised if blacks turn away in disgust. The difficulty is not with the reconciliation — forgiveness question itself but with the people asking it ... They who are responsible for the walls of hostility, racism and hatred want to know whether the victims are ready to forgive and forget — without changing the balance of power. (Cone 1997, p. 207)

Social justice is about changing the balance of power, about setting things right, about restoring the rights of the oppressed. Those in power, however, do not relinquish their power readily, just because they are confronted with angry victims. The political will to change the balance of power requires a change of heart. The deeper dimension of social justice involves more than rights; it involves listening to stories; hearing the truth; joining in the struggle; acknowledging that, in the past, justice has been offered on the terms of the oppressors. Indigenous people have not only been the victims of injustice. As victims they have also been blamed for their own plight. Lisa Bellear cries,

> In my defence and let me state I
> emphatically believe that I have not
> had an opportunity to respond on
> equal terms with my detractors
> accusers. Tell me is this your
> system of democratic justice. I
> demand fairness. I am innocent.
> (Reed-Gilbert 1997, p. 3)

Social justice involves joining the victims and discovering they are not victims; they are suffering, resisting, searching human beings. It is this principle of justice that must inform the search for reconciliation, a principle that probes beyond rights to resistance. Social justice is a painful rebalancing of power that takes place in stages throughout the reconciliation process. I agree here with Wink.

> Many people think of reconciliation as something that
> comes about only after justice is done. Some
> liberationists bridle at all talk of reconciliation during
> the conflict. No doubt they have seen church leaders
> disguise a bogus neutrality behind calls for
> reconciliation. Nevertheless, nonviolent activists have
> repeatedly demonstrated the value of reaching across

the divide while the struggle for justice is going on. Both
sides have to live together after the end of the conflict
... Those who insist on waiting till justice is done to be
reconciled may never be reconciled, for justice is seldom
done completely. (Wink 1998, pp. 21–2)

Wink's position should not be read to mean that justice is
to be relegated to the margin or background. Far from it.
Rather, it means that justice is not a set of political acts
which can be performed to create equality and balance
power. Rather, justice must be embraced as part of the
ongoing struggle to overcome the wrongs of the past, and
build new bonds of community. It remains true that

[t]here can be no reconciliation without justice. Both
the Torres Strait Islander people and the Aboriginal
people will continue to judge the process of
reconciliation against the extent to which justice is
delivered. (Council 1993b, session 1.7)

The identity principle

The identity principle asserts that the cultural identity of
both parties in a conflict, especially that of the oppressed
party, is to be valued equally and not negated as alien or
'other'. Miroslav Volf has explored this principle in
connection with the upheavals and atrocities in Bosnia.

Various kinds of cultural 'cleansings' demand of us to
place *identity and otherness at the center of theological
reflection* on social realities ... [A]longside these three
(rights, justice and ecology), space should be made for
a fourth — identity and otherness — and all four
should be understood in relation to the other. (Volf
1996, pp. 17–18)

Given the history of treating Aboriginal peoples as so
'other' that they were regarded as closer to apes than humans
and their possession of a soul was in question, the

application of this principle cannot be avoided. The strength and spirituality of Aboriginal culture has long been suppressed. And even now, many non-indigenous Australians only admire those areas of Aboriginal culture which can be exploited in the tourist trade. For reconciliation to mean more than a tolerance of 'tribal ways and wisdom' that is motivated by self-interest, I believe we immigrant Australians need to understand and value the mythic, spiritual and ritual tradition of Aboriginal peoples as integral to their identity. Their Aboriginal identity is 'in with and under' their land — wherever that may be in Australia. To be an Aboriginal Australian is to have a specific kinship with a piece of this country.

Given the debilitating government policy of assimilation that was proclaimed officially in 1937 — but operative long before then — the identity principle is extremely significant. The aim of assimilation policies was that 'the Aboriginal problem would ultimately disappear — the people would lose their identity within the wider community' (ATSIC 1998, p. 10). To uphold the principle of identity is to honour Aboriginal people, not only as human beings like other human beings, but also as indigenous Australians who are distinctive and different in ways that make their contribution to the spirit and identity of Australia of great worth.

The forgiveness factor

Reconciliation, unlike many peace processes, takes seriously how the relationship has been broken and seeks to restore the relationship, not only legally and politically as issues of justice, but also morally — and I believe spiritually — to facilitate the healing of the spirit. Healing a community usually involves a process — a series of rites that bring people together. The forgiveness factor is an essential part of the healing process as the Joseph precedent illustrates.

It is my experience in the Australian context that the forgiveness factor has played, and can continue to play, a key role in the healing process. Forgiveness heals past hurts, heals past history, heals the wounds of alienation and enables parties to embrace each other again as fellow human beings with a just future together. That is the goal of the Truth and Reconciliation Commission in South Africa. As Archbishop Tutu, who was the head of this commission, said,

> [o]ne lesson we should be able to teach the world, and that we should be able to teach the people of Bosnia, Rwanda and Burundi, is that we are ready to forgive. (Henderson 1996, p. xix)

The words of an Aboriginal mother — one of the stolen generation — also suggests that forgiveness is still possible. Her words are recorded on a rock beside the 'Fountain of Tears' sculpture in Adelaide.

> And every morning as the sun came up the whole family would wail. They did that for 32 years until they saw me again. Who can imagine what a mother went through? But you have to learn to forgive.

Forgiveness in the social domain, if it is to have any healing force, needs to incorporate rituals of reconciliation — even if these actions are not called rituals. Increasingly, governments, institutions, church bodies and community groups across the globe perform rituals of reconciliation as a fundamental part of the process. In some cases, these rituals are performed in a religious context. More often they are secular acts. A spiritual dimension, however, is usually discernible in these rituals, especially where the forgiveness factor is prominent.

These rites may include public confessions, public apologies, public expressions of sorrow, public acts of repentance and public pleas for forgiveness. These penitentiary rites may be performed at meaningful sacred places or sites of past atrocities. Significantly, however, they are not one-off events but are celebrated over an extended period of time as the community comes to terms with its wounded soul.

One or both alienated parties may make a formal response, accepting the apology or confession of the other party — without using the specific language of forgiveness. Actual words of forgiveness, however, together with an assurance from both parties to work together — as equals — for a better future, represent a publicly recognisable stage in the reconciliation process.

Often a common symbol emerges, one with which both parties can identify. Both affirm this symbol as profound and meaningful — a symbol of their common past, especially their suffering in the past. Through that symbol both parties may come together to say, 'we are sorry', and 'we forgive'.

Forgiveness is not a word spoken once and then forgotten. Reconciliation is not 'forgive and forget'. Forgiveness is a painful process — painful for those like myself who learn progressively the sins of our people against indigenous Australians, and painful for those who have been abused so long and now reach out to affirm the descendants of those who abused their people. Each time the forgiveness factor comes into play, a barrier is overcome and the process of reconciliation is advanced.

This truth was brought home to me when the local community gathered at the site of the former Colebrook Home. The act of handing over sorry books to the surviving stolen children from Colebrook Home, our communal expression of sorrow and regret, and the public word of forgiveness may not have ended the reconciliation process, but these actions have given the process new impetus. That moment was, as Wink puts it, 'a flash of divine in the world's darkness' (Wink 1998, p. 29).

The suffering factor

Reconciliation involves suffering which is also part of the healing process. Exploring stories of past injustices and alienation will inevitably uncover a history of suffering — often so brutal that most of us would prefer not to face it.

Facing the wrongs of the past, struggling for justice and mediating healing will involve 'suffering through' the process of reconciliation. Admittedly this 'suffering through' may be different for both parties, but without it the end result is likely to be a false reconciliation, a temporary truce, and ultimately a mockery of mutual communal respect.

Christians identify with the suffering of God, regardless of their cultural identity. For Christians, the suffering of God is revealed in the cross of Jesus Christ, and the cross becomes the instrument of reconciliation and healing. In the conflict of the early church between Jews and Gentiles outlined above, identifying with the suffering of God on the cross reconciled both groups to each other and to God. That suffering became redemptive for their community.

As we explore the story of suffering in the Australian context, as we search for the Australian soul in our past, as we seek healing between alienated Australians in the reconciliation process, we will also search the stories of suffering for symbols that might mediate healing. This search involves 'reliving' the various stories of suffering in our history and asking whether these moments strike more than chords of sympathy. Do they express a suffering with which we identify? Is there an event that brings us closer as we relive it together in rite, memory or song? Or, in Christian language, is the suffering of God discernible in our common Australian history?

We could perhaps identify other principles and factors that are involved in the Australian reconciliation scenario. If, however, we find ways to maintain the principles identified above and implement them throughout the process, we will keep alive the vision of reconciliation for Australia. If we seek justice, unearth the hidden stories, respect identity and pursue healing, we may in the process discover more than social community and respect — we may discern the contours of the Australian soul.

CHAPTER 3

TELLING THE STORY

For me, reconciliation means you start at day one,
Invasion Day. (Pryor 1998, p. 172)

The task of this chapter is to apply the truth principle set out in the previous chapter and retell the stories of Australia's past from the perspective of the indigenous peoples of Australia. To do this I have selected seven stories from our collective history. Each is representative of particular grave injustices perpetrated against Aboriginal people: dispossession, genocide, massacre, dehumanisation, destruction of culture, desecration, and assimilation. These stories also form the basis for the rites of healing in the Appendix.

Telling the story

To overcome the alienation between indigenous and immigrant Australians, I believe that we must first recount the story of what happened in our collective history as Australians. Those moved by the dream of technology or the vision of economic progress may have eyes only for the future. To pursue the goal of reconciliation, I believe, requires that we apply the truth principle, that is, enable both sides to tell their story of what happened — especially those whose story has been suppressed by the dominant culture.

Relating the stories and empathising with those stories are two different things. To help me empathise with what happened to my Aboriginal brothers and sisters I searched for a piece of history in my own past. I looked for something beyond my control to help me understand what it was like when 'what happened' is distorted by a biased storyteller. I looked for a similar moment of my history that had been largely ignored because it too challenges our national ideal, our identity as mates, and the belief that we will always give people a fair go. I found an example in what happened to me and my community during the Second World War.

Ironically, my most vivid memory is related to a tabloid paper known as *The Truth*. Early in the war, an edition was issued with bold letters across the front page: NAZI SETTLEMENT NEAR HAMILTON. The faces of local Lutheran pastors were plastered across the tabloid as if they were the ringleaders of a Nazi spy ring operating among the Lutheran community.

As a volatile youth I was incensed, especially since I was a fifth generation Australian and my community was actively supporting the war effort. I was being taught by the local media to hate the Huns without really making any connection with my own German ancestry. That story was enough to alienate me from my school friends. I did not relish being asked whether I was a German spy. No one ever apologised. After considerable pressure from the local church community *The Truth* expressed its regrets — buried in small print on a back page. I knew then that being vilified in public because of my ethnic origins can be cruel and vicious, especially when no one faces the truth later.

As individuals and communities, we tend to force things that do not fit with our understanding of what happened down into our subconscious. We hide the great lie of our history. Nevertheless, writes Villa-Vincencio, the

> truth of the matter is, however, that we do not destroy the reality of the past. The unremembered past endures. This is that part of the truth that each section of society is required to face. It can do so thoughtfully and carefully, or risk the possibility that it will erupt in an uncontrollable manner. Suppressed and forgotten truth is part of the inclusive truth that must be uncovered if a polarised society is to be united in a healing process.
> (Villa-Vincencio 1997, p. 36)

The process of telling the stories of what happened must continue if we, as immigrant Australians, are eventually to accept the wrongs and lies of the past as an integral part of Australia's heritage. The ugly picture of what happened in the past may take us some time to grasp, publicly acknowledge and internalise, but doing so is vital if we, as Aboriginal and non-Aboriginal peoples, are to be reconciled. To suppress the truth principle is to numb our conscience and to cover up the stories is to provide a haven for racism. Making Australia's collective history public truth means searching for stories of our soul, lost memories of who we all are as Australians.

Invasion bay: *dispossession*

When Governor Phillip and his party anchored in Sydney Cove, they hoisted the Union Jack, drank toasts to their patron, King George III, fired volleys of musketry and gave three cheers. The entire population of the First Fleet, it seems, assembled before the flag on 7 February 1788, and took formal possession of the colony on behalf of the British monarch. From that day, Australia ostensibly belonged to Britain.

The story of the landing of the First Fleet delighted us in primary school. We re-enacted the event in the schoolyard.

We drew a line across the gravel where the ships landed and the governor came ashore with his colourful entourage to claim the land for the home country. We saluted the flag as it was raised on the flagpole and sounded a cannon made of forty-four-gallon drums. We revelled in the toast that we raised when we hailed king and country with our tin cups.

Even though my heritage was German Lutheran, we were patriotic followers of the King of England. The school tuned our hearts to love England. It seemed only fitting that when the British arrived they should display their glory and assume control. Any indigenous Australians in sight retreated into the bush and disappeared from the scene — and from our history. As far as we were concerned, they played no part in the establishment of the colony.

Henry Reynolds asks, what really happened when the British laid claim to the sovereignty over New South Wales and the rest of Australia on 7 February?

> Australians are so familiar with the events of January and February 1788 that they have lost sight of the ability to see how extraordinary the claim was ...
> As many as half a million people, living in several hundred tribal groupings, in occupation of even the most inhospitable corners of the continent, had, in a single instant, been dispossessed. From that apocalyptic moment forward they were technically trespassers on Crown land even though many of them would not see a white man for another thirty, another fifty years ...
> It was a stunning takeover. It would have dazzled even the lions of the modern business world. (Reynolds 1992, p. 8)

This dazzling takeover, this massive dispossession, was justified by the 'right of discovery'. Captain Cook and other explorers had supposedly 'earned' the land for Britain by 'discovering' it, a privilege reserved for the Europeans. We know, of course, that the Europeans were not the first to discover Australia. We know, too, that the land was not empty (*terra nullius*). Indigenous Australians had been custodians of this country for thousands of years. The truth for these indigenous inhabitants is that the action of Governor Phillip was tantamount to an invasion. Sydney Cove is, in reality, invasion bay.

It is also true that from the beginning there was what Reynolds has called a 'whispering in our hearts', a voice stirring our consciences to question Britain's right to invade, dispossess and kill. Reynolds cites the voices of humanitarians such as Robinson and Threlkeld, who challenged the policy of the early settlement to the point where a Sydney barrister claimed that if Robinson's views were accepted the colonists would 'have nothing to do but to take ship and go home' (Reynolds 1998, p. 19).

The Black War: *genocide*

At school we were told, with considerable pride and gratitude, that Australia was different from other countries in so many ways. One distinctive feature of Australia's 'brief history', it was claimed, is that no wars have ever been fought on Australian soil. The Japanese may have bombed Darwin, but we have had no continental wars like those of the Europeans, and no civil war like that of the Americans.

That assertion is, of course, patently false. There were a series of wars in almost every state of Australia between the British or the immigrant Australians and the indigenous people of this land. Grassby and Hill (1988) call the conflict in New South Wales the 'Hundred Years War'.

> The period from the arrival in 1788 of the First Fleet to establish the first English settlement in Australia to the withdrawal of the last garrison of British soldiers in 1870 was marked by constant warfare. The heirs of the 2000 generations who had held the continent in trust

for over 40,000 years fought and died in defence of their land for even longer, the last massacre of the first Australians being recorded in 1928. (Grassby & Hill 1988, p. 34)

Of all the wars fought against the Australian Aborigines, the Black War in Tasmania was perhaps the most inhumane. The Black War reached its heights in the 1830s and resulted in the near genocide of the indigenous peoples. The early settlers in Tasmania were mostly ex-prisoners from New South Wales who initially paid 'rent' to the Tasmanians with tea, tobacco and dogs. Early coexistence included settlers receiving wives from the Tasmanians. However, as Grassby and Hill write, the

> whites were more interested in Tasmanian children as a source of labour and embarked on widespread kidnapping of both boys and girls from their families. By 1816 the Tasmanians were forced to defend themselves and launched a series of attacks designed to drive the foreigners into the sea. (Grassby & Hill 1988, p. 54)

After several years of local raids by settlers and counter-attacks by indigenous groups, Governor Arthur, in the spring of 1830, planned a joint offensive with a regiment of soldiers, police, prisoners and settlers. They formed a human chain across the settled districts of Tasmania. This human chain, known as the 'black line', moved relentlessly southwards for three weeks. Those who eluded the net were persuaded by George Robinson, a devious diplomat, to surrender. Fewer than 200 indigenous Tasmanians from the settled districts survived; all the survivors had been wounded.

When the remnants of these Tasmanian indigenous people were exiled to Flinders Island in Bass Strait, the land had been cleared of 'natives'. The process of genocide was almost complete. Among those who survived was the famous Truganini, who came to be known as 'the last Tasmanian'. Today we know that there are several thousand descendants of these indigenous Tasmanians still resisting — albeit peacefully — the total clearance of indigenous peoples from their land by the so-called black line (Grassby & Hill 1988, p. 58).

The inhumane policy that the authorities perpetrated in Tasmania still has the power to shock contemporary Australians; it also shocked people of the time. The fate of the Tasmanians — 'shot like crows' — was publicised in England at the height of the antislavery crusade. The brutality, bloodshed and near genocide, it was said, 'left an indelible stain' on the British government of the Australian colonies. A remorseful Governor Arthur reported what he called the necessity of 'driving a simple but warlike, and, as it appears now, nobleminded race from its hunting grounds'. According to Reynolds, the

> Black War in Tasmania played a similar role [to the slave rebellion in Jamaica] in convincing people that the method of colonisation needs a radical change ... If the Tasmanian experience were to be repeated in the rest of Australia the prospect was daunting. A few years of conflict had left 1000 dead (800 blacks and 200 whites), and caused enormous property loss, insecurity and collapse of investor confidence. (Reynolds 1992, pp. 88–9)

Even the outcry against this brutal policy did not prevent later conflicts and massacres on the mainland. Did these Tasmanians die in vain? The futility and evil of the Black War technique as a means of colonisation was recognised by many. Hopefully today we recognise that colonisation is itself a form of warfare that regards indigenous peoples as the inevitable victims of progress.

Feeding stations: *dehumanisation*

As a youth from the Western District of Victoria, I grew up in woolsheds. My community was proud that its farmers were contributing to the prosperity of a country that 'rode on the sheep's back'. We all knew that John Macarthur was the first sheep king, and that sheep stations across Australia were indebted to him for bringing the best Merino sheep from Spain in 1805 in order to establish the wool industry in Australia.

We knew little of the headstrong ways of Macarthur, or of his conflicts with the authorities. As far as we were concerned, he was the inspiration for turning Australia into a wealthy land divided into thousands of sheep stations. What we did not learn, however, was that the transformation of Australia's landscape into a panorama of pastoral allotments and leases had disastrous consequences. The spacious regions of Australia's inland were progressively surveyed and settled or occupied by ambitious squatters. They were usually systematically cleared of unwanted life — whether animal, vegetable or 'Aboriginal'.

The sheep industry, perhaps more than any other, led to the dispossession and destruction of Aboriginal communities. Kangaroos and other Australian fauna were killed without any consideration for the indigenous communities who depended upon them for sustenance. Sheep were God's gift to Australia. The hidden story is that many of our farming ancestors treated the Aboriginal owners of the land as trespassers who could be shot at will.

How many of us know that, in spite of this treatment, many sheep and cattle stations were dependent on cheap Aboriginal labour for stockmen and workers at the homestead? As one Queensland Aboriginal elder said to me, 'Australia rode on the backs of Aborigines, not sheep.'

How many of us realise that what George Robinson called 'a complete system of expulsion and extermination' was, in fact, denounced by early humanitarians as immoral and evil? As early as 1841, George Robinson visited the Western District of Victoria and discovered that the Aboriginal people had already been dispossessed of their traditional lands. Reynolds' analysis illustrates the frustration of men like Robinson.

> While staying overnight with squatters he learned of the prevailing attitudes. He recorded a breakfast-time conversation with a Mr H—. Robinson broached the subject of the rights of the natives to the soil. His host would hear none of it, saying that he would 'not give in to that' because it was never intended that 'a few miserable savages were to have this fine country'. Robinson observed that H. ran 7000 sheep and paid £70 per annum to the government and for that trifle he held 'half an English county'.
> (Reynolds 1998, p. 50)

Most of the Aboriginal Australians who died last century were not killed in battles or massacres. They perished because white settlers cleared the scrub that was the source of their bush tucker. Native animal and bird life were replaced by sheep and cattle. Aborigines and farm animals competed for the same waterholes. Natural food supplies disappeared and local Aborigines were forced to depend on rations dispensed by white settlers, missionaries or government officials at 'feeding stations'. Those rations were mainly second-grade sugar, potatoes and flour. Dispossession meant destroying the 'bread of life' which had served these custodians of life in the land for thousands of years. Aboriginal peoples, often malnourished when without access to their traditional foods, had no immunity to diseases brought by the European invaders. Smallpox and measles almost wiped out some communities; Aboriginal health was much better prior to colonisation.

This dependency on the white invaders for food made the indigenous peoples of Australia even more vulnerable. When crises arose and racism erupted, local settlers or police sometimes laced the flour with arsenic, or poisoned the waterholes. In the struggle against the Wiradjuri, who fought to kept their traditional lands in the lower Murrumbidgee, this technique was employed as a weapon of war.

At Poisoned Waterholes Creek near Ganmain, bags of flour were laced with arsenic and the water poisoned. A large party of more than 100 Wiradjuri arrived to camp, and within hours men, women and children were writhing in agony. Armed and mounted men then swept down on the camp from all sides, firing until the dead choked in the creek. (Grassby & Hill 1988, p. 44)

Sad to say, the manipulation of food was also seen as the vehicle to destroy traditional ways and civilise indigenous peoples. As the clerk to the Resident Magistrate at Port Lincoln wrote in 1832,

I am decidedly of the opinion that the stomach is the organ which should first be attempted as the medium of civilisation. Full and regular meals gradually disqualify them for the precarious life of the bush, and the incessant efforts which the demands of nature impose … Boiled wheat and sugar, or bread and milk, twice a day, and 'bullocky' or 'sheepy' once, are most effective civilisers. (Mattingley 1988, p. 20)

Rations were a reward for good behaviour and compliance; withholding food was a punishment for acts of resistance. Rations were supplied in many regions until the 1960s. Even with the best of intentions, government and mission bodies dished out as rations to Aboriginal people processed foods that were alien to them, and tantamount to poison.

Islands of exile: *destruction of culture*

I vaguely remember local rhetoric about the noble work of a particular office of the Australian government whose role was to 'protect Aborigines'. The so-called 'Protector of Aborigines' was to consider the interests of Aboriginal people in relation to the policies and programs of the nation. The idea was that someone had to protect Aborigines from themselves, from their pagan culture, and from their misguided ways. The church and the state were viewed as the 'father who knows best'.

I have since learned that in Queensland, for example, the goal of the 'protector' was to erase Aboriginal culture and replace it with civilised culture — British or Christian, or both. One of the policies was popularly called the 'Dog Act', because under it Aboriginal people said they were treated like dogs. This policy involved gathering Aboriginal groups from diverse language groups and locating them in settlements, reserves and missions of various kinds. These 'new homes' were a form of exile far from their home country and kin. In exile, Aboriginal people were forbidden to speak their own languages; they were forced to speak English, the language of their oppressors. I recall one of the Rainbow Spirit Elders telling me that, when he was five, he and his mother were thrown in prison because she dared to comfort him in her own language. Or, in the words of Wadjullarbinna, who was sent to a Doomadgee reserve run by Plymouth Brethren,

> [m]y sister and I had our mouths washed out with soap
> for speaking our language. The face-washer, they
> rubbed soap on it and they got us and they put it in our
> mouths. Terrible you know, to have soap up your nose
> and your mouth just because you're talking; we
> couldn't speak a word of English you know. We had to
> learn English and we had to live like white people

because 'your mother and father's way is heathenism'.
I didn't understand what heathenism was until a lot
later on, when I left that reserve and I got a hold of a
dictionary, but I knew it must have been bad because of
the tone of their voice. (Rintoul 1993, p. 141)

Wadjullarbinna's story is a painful reminder of the tragic
plight of many women in North Queensland, especially so-
called 'half-castes'. She recounts that her mother refused to
explain why she was treated differently, and how at her birth
she survived being killed as a 'half-caste'.

One day I found out. I went to another granny and I
said, 'Granny tell me why I'm like I am — half white?'
And she tell me then, 'It really bad but I tell you. White
men been come into our tribe and take at gunpoint the
women they want and they just used them, and if a
blackfella get up to stop them they just fire shot and
blackfella got shot — a lot of them got shot — or they
just make them go back and they just take the women.'
(Rintoul 1993, p. 144)
When I was born, the midwife was so scared she put
me out in the antheap to be just ... They knew that
somebody would probably try to kill me because I was
half white. I still had my cord on me and they put me
out and I was in the bushes. And one young boy, about
sixteen or seventeen, was getting bark for his mother
and he went over to have a look and he found me. The
ants were all over me and eating me. I had to be
cleaned up. (Rintoul 1993, p. 145)

The Protector of Aborigines sent indigenous Australians
from diverse language regions — often in chains — to the
following places of exile: Yarrabah, Cherbourg, Wujal Wujal,
Hopevale and Palm Island. Dormitory life — the norm in
many of these places — was harsh and tyrannical. Nellie
Sheridan was taken to a girl's dormitory in Cherbourg when

she was ten and describes it as really cruel. The doors of the dormitory were locked and a high barbed-wire fence surrounded the buildings. 'We had to sleep on the bare floor: we had no mattress. All we lived on was damper, brownie, pea soup and molasses. We would put fat and salt on the damper.' Nellie worked for forty-five years at the camp but was never paid. She still lives in Cherbourg (Rintoul 1993, pp. 197–199).

Palm Island is remembered as the harshest of all these places of exile. The threat of sending someone to Palm Island was the heaviest sanction an officer from the Department of Aboriginal and Islander Affairs could invoke (Horton 1994, p. 840). Palm Island was known as a 'place of punishment' for Aborigines in missions or reserves who misbehaved, or stood up for people's rights. Carl Wyles remembers how the mission bell rang at nine each evening to summon all indoors. Those caught outside could be put in the cooler.

> Sometimes you'd get about six people in one cell,
> sleeping on the floor. It was about ten feet by ten feet.
> You got six people in there and you all got to lie
> together. And you've got the old pan there, the toilet
> pan, in one corner. You know the smell of the pan.
> If someone opened the pan to have a pee or something
> like it would go right through the cell ... When they
> gave you the deportation order, you had to go. It was
> bad them days ... They used to have us under the
> Aborigines Protection Act, but they weren't protecting
> us: they were robbing us. (Rintoul 1993, pp. 208–209)

In spite of the efforts of missions and reserves to cut Aborigines off from their traditional culture, and civilise them, the culture often survived underground. Or, as Wadjullarbinna says, '[o]ur culture was intact, but we had to do it really sneaky, don't let the missionary know' (Rintoul 1993, p. 141). Hopevale was one of the missions where people from many language groups survived under a strong mission program. George Rosendale, one of the Rainbow

Spirit Elders at Hopevale, related to me once the way in which a spiritual link was maintained with the original country from which his family was exiled. When George was born under a tree, his mother took the afterbirth and the umbilical cord and buried it in the ground — not to dispose of it, but so that the spirit or life in the blood could, through the land, link up with the country of their ancestors far away. From these stories immigrant Australians must recognise not only that Australian authorities sought to exile Aborigines and erase their culture, but also that in spite of these organised efforts to destroy their culture, Aboriginal people used techniques of resistance. Ongoing resistance has enabled many of them to keep their culture alive — even in exile.

The last post: *massacre*

Until recent years I had never heard that massacres were periodic events in Australia's past. Yet massacres are an integral part of our communal history and they have scarred our Australian soul.

In almost every small town in Australia there is a monument to those who gave their lives for this country in various wars. Few and far between are monuments to the indigenous Australians who gave their lives for this land — people who were massacred in cold blood. The monument at Cloncurry, on the border between the Kalkadoon and Mitakoodi, is a reminder of the massacres in that region. The plaque on one side reads,

YOU WHO PASS BY
ARE NOW ENTERING THE ANCIENT
TRIBAL LANDS OF THE KALKADOON
DISPOSSESSED BY THE EUROPEAN
HONOUR THEIR NAME
BE BROTHERS AND SISTERS TO
THEIR DESCENDANTS

Sad to say this monument has been desecrated. Would we do the same to Anzac monuments? Many Australians have yet to face the reality that indigenous people did die for this land. They deserve to be honoured in some way — not necessarily with Western types of monuments — so that all Australians can continue to acknowledge the Aboriginal story as integral to our shared past.

It is not my intention to recount the many massacres in Australia's recent history. I shall focus on the last one recorded because it illustrates not only that these atrocities belong to our recent past, but also because the leader of the expedition was an Anzac, a man whom we might have expected to appreciate the value of lives being given for the land.

During 1928, a drought in Central Australia brought the Walpiri and Aranda in conflict with the pastoralists. Water was scarce and bush tucker was hard to find. Cattle killing increased as hunger grew. Rumours of black vengeance were rife and the manager of Coniston station called for police protection. Henry Reynolds describes the course of events that led to the Coniston massacre in August of that year.

> an already threatening atmosphere worsened dramatically when on 7 August the dingo trapper and local identity Fred Brooks was killed and his mutilated body thrust into an enlarged rabbit burrow. He had taken an Aboriginal woman from a camp beside a soak at Coniston station and had refused to return her or to supply the gifts expected as part of the exchange. But in the eyes of the white community nothing could excuse or extenuate the guilt which was not individual but collective. The cry went up, unanimous and ancestral — the black must be taught a lesson they will never forget. The scene was set for the last official punitive expedition and one of its most brutal and unrestrained. (Reynolds 1998, pp. 191–2)

The police reprisal expedition was led by a Gallipoli veteran and a tough bushman, Mounted Constable George Murray. He left Coniston Station with eight armed horsemen on 16 August, and returned to a hero's welcome in Alice Springs on 1 September. As many as seventy Aborigines may have been slaughtered on the expedition; the number remains uncertain even though no effort was made to hide the massacre, as in some instances, by burning or burying the dead.

The Coniston massacre is generally considered the last official massacre of Aboriginal people in Australia and illustrates the fierce racism rampant in Central Australia at the time. According to the *Northern Territory Times*, many settlers 'preferred a dead black to a live one'. According to Reynolds, the 'Coniston killings revealed a state of mind which found acceptable the fact that the Aborigine was "regarded as dirt" who could be "shot wholesale on an unproven hypothesis"' (Reynolds 1998, p. 195).

Reynolds estimates that 20,000 blacks were killed before Federation. They all died for this land. How shall we remember them? Should we not embrace this story as publicly as we have the Anzac legend? Or shall we continue to expunge their memory from our Australian soul?

Maralinga: *desecration*

Between 1952 and 1956 the British, with the approval of the Australian government, exploded twelve nuclear weapons in three Australian locations — the Monte Bello Islands off the north-west coast, Emu and Maralinga in South Australia. At that time I was being challenged by the issues of a college curriculum. Maralinga, however, was not an issue for us — ethically or theologically. We were assured by the government that the Aboriginal Australians living in the so-called 'prohibited zone' around the test sites of Emu and Maralinga had all been safely relocated in nearby settlements. Many of them were taken, rather fortuitously we Lutherans thought, to the Lutheran mission settlement at Koonibba. There they would get food, education and religion. We sincerely believed the move was in their best interests.

How wrong we were! All life and land in these areas became contaminated; Aboriginal Australians both inside and outside the prohibited zone were exposed to radioactive contamination and fallout. The 1985 royal commission into these tests indicated that several of the bombs were exploded in weather conditions considered unsafe for people outside the prohibited zone. Little is known of the effects of this radiation on the Aboriginal people because most of their stories have been suppressed. Some, such as Yami Lester, were blinded by the fallout.

Aborigines at Wallatinna reported a big 'black mist' coming from the direction of Emu. This black radioactive cloud brought sickness and death to the people. The 'red sands' in the area, of which the people were proud, became 'poisoned' and turned grey. The Aboriginal people in these lands suffered more than dislocation; they suffered dehumanisation because political leaders were willing to sacrifice Aboriginal lives for an alleged 'greater good'. Their spirits were crushed in a nuclear power game. In recent years a few Aboriginal Australians are returning to the fringes of the prohibited zone. Their crushed spirits are rising again with the multi-million dollar clean-up of the nuclear particles by the British.

Why did all this happen? The attitude of the government is summed up by Howard Beale, the Federal Minister of Supply at the time.

> It is a challenge to Australian men [sic] to show that the pioneering spirit of their forefathers who developed our country is still the driving force of achievement ...
> England has the bomb and the know-how; we have the open spaces, much technical skill and great willingness to help the motherland. Between us we will help to

build the defences of the free world, and make historic
advances in harnessing the forces of nature. (Royal
Commission into British Nuclear Tests in Australia
1985, p. 15)

The enormity of this action can perhaps be grasped if we
imagine the government today giving the Americans at Pine
Gap permission to trial missiles with chemical warheads in
Australia. These missiles would target the cathedrals and
parklands in each of the main cities. All worshippers and
wanderers would be removed from the designated sites. The
exercise would be performed to demonstrate our defence
capabilities — to keep Australia free. The desecrated areas
would be testimony to our technological skills and our
democratic ideals.

The truth about Maralinga and similar places is that the
desecration was more than contamination by nuclear fallout,
which is something we non-residents can perhaps grasp. The
deeper desecration was the pollution of sacred sites, sacred
ancestor trails, and sacred land. This land was the indigenous
people's spiritual home, their link with the creator spirits in
the earth, their sacred ground of being. To remove them from
their spiritual roots was evil enough; to pollute their
sanctuary with a 'white man poison' was doubly immoral.

This desecration and destruction of the spiritual places of
indigenous Australians happened throughout Australia.
Maralinga is but a brutal climax to a longstanding policy.
This event recalls again for me the incisive prophet Jeremiah
who speaks of Judah as the one who 'greatly polluted the
land' and deserved to be expelled from the land (Jeremiah
3:1, 9). For me, immigrant Australians are like those who
polluted that land. Whatever other associations Maralinga
stirs in our collective memories, immigrant Australians
devalued the indigenous people and their traditional lands to
such an extent that the government authorities were willing
to sacrifice both to meet a misguided political goal.

Fountain of Tears: *assimilation*

Colebrook Home was an isolated place in Eden Hills, South Australia. Residents in the community were told that this house, and others like it, were orphanages for unfortunate Aboriginal children who had lost their parents. The community saw these children walk in neat rows to Blackwood Primary School each day. These children, however, were not allowed to play with non-residents after school. Life in Colebrook Home was very strict, but outsiders had no idea of what really happened inside. The government and the institution hid the stories of these children from the public.

In 1997, *Bringing Them Home*, the Report of the National Inquiry into the Separation of Aboriginal and Torres Strait Islander Children from Their Families, was released. This report tells the tragic story of how Aboriginal children were forcibly removed — 'stolen' — from their parents and placed in public institutions or private homes. The hidden stories were exposed as these 'stolen children' told the inquiry about the painful experiences of Aboriginal parents and children subjected to the misguided government policy of racial assimilation. Chapter 8 illustrates further the suffering of these indigenous Australians.

The children who were specially targeted by this policy were the so-called 'half-castes'. The government's aim was to make them white, and assimilate them into white society. We also need to know that there were those who saw the policy as evil, and opposed it or found a way to negate it. Joyleen Abbott remembers what happened to children like herself.

There is one half-caste left in Henbury, they been after
me all the time, but I always hide. One time at Henbury
Mr Frinney, the Welfare from Alice Springs, and
MacKinnon the policemen and Ted Strehlow come
and they ask my mother, 'Where is your daughter?'
She doesn't say anything. Strehlow is standing there

and I'm hiding inside the humpy ... And my mum went
'Come on, come out, the policeman want you'. I cry
and cry and cry. I don't like come out and Mum bring
me to see Strehlow is standing there.
'What are you going to do with this half-caste?' [*sic*]
Strehlow said.
'Take her away.'
'No', Strehlow reckon. 'You can't touch this kid. How
many people have gone from here and never come back
to their parents? This girl's gotta go to Hermannsburg.
You don't touch her now.' (Rintoul 1993, p. 109)

On 31 March 1998 a stone monument was dedicated at
the site of the former Colebrook Home where stolen children
were institutionalised until 1971. Entitled 'Fountain of
Tears', this monument symbolises in a dramatic way the
sorrow of the Aboriginal parents who lost their children. The
water from the fountain flows down from a coolamon — a
hollowed piece of wood used to carry babies — over the
faces of six Aboriginal people into a pool of water
symbolising the tears of the parents. The water from that
pool was used in a healing ritual for those present at the
dedication. The ritual included an apology for wrongs
committed against the children and families of the stolen
generation, and an expression of forgiveness from Lowitja
O'Donoghue and others who were once institutionalised in
Colebrook. All those present then joined hands until we were
all linked up with one person who placed her hands in the
fountain of tears. This fountain is already regarded by some
as a sacred place for those who seek spiritual strength.

The story of Colebrook Home reveals that there has
been a hidden history of forcible removal and stealing of
young Aboriginal people by a racist government policy. This
is also a story of opposition and anguish that has long been
suppressed. We must now acknowledge both stories as part
of who we are as Australians.

The search

Facing what happened in our collective past is an integral part of our search for who we are. Our European ancestors have perpetrated evils which, I hope, still have the power to horrify us today. We are a people with a shameful past, a people who cannot assume the moral high ground as if we have a single noble heritage. Our soul has been numbed by crimes that shame us. These stories reveal that though some voices were raised against these ills, Aboriginal people suffered and died. Their stories are also part of our communal heritage; their courageous pain and loss now contribute to who we are. Our heritage embraces both ugly invaders and indigenous martyrs, silenced protesters and silent exiles.

CHAPTER 4

THE POISON OF RACISM

Racism is the denial of the worth of some persons because of their 'race' and culture. It is a sin which undermines the human worth of Aboriginal and Torres Strait Islander people, 'threatening us as if we were not made in the image of God. It prevents us from fulfilling our potential. It deprives us of our land.' The first action required of the church is *to destroy the credibility of racism*. From the Manifesto of Charles Harris (Delphin-Stanford & Brown 1994, p. 13)

This chapter tackles the question of racism as an ideology that, like a poison, led immigrant Australians to justify committing the seven sins outlined in the previous chapter. I first explore my own racist heritage as a means of discerning the nature of racism and summarising the features of racism as a sin. I analyse briefly how the concept of 'race' developed and examine the force of racism within the Christian church. To illustrate the poisonous nature of racism I demonstrate the connection between racism and some of the injustices which followed. Finally, I focus on the need to recognise, confess and remove the plague of racism that still infects the soul of Australia.

My racist background

Who are these immigrant Australians, these people who committed the atrocities and evils described in the previous chapter? As descendants of these Australians, who are we today? What kind of power led us to perpetrate such barbaric deeds?

After struggling for years with the bitter truth of my heritage, I have come to the realisation that racism has been a primal force in Australia's history. By 'primal' I mean that force which gives rise to — and justifies — the long history of wrongs perpetrated against the indigenous people of this land. If Australians are to experience authentic reconciliation, this deep-seated force must be exposed for what it is and named as a sin. While 'sin' may not be a popular word today, I can think of no more apt expression. Racism is not merely a wrong, an injustice, a false attitude or a prejudice — it is a sin, a virus, that has poisoned the minds of immigrant Australians.

My own understanding of racism as a poisonous power came after years of painful experience. I imbibed my racist beliefs from an early age. In the small rural community where I lived, we rarely saw indigenous Australians. They had been totally dispossessed by our European ancestors — including my own forebears. One of the few times we did see Aborigines was during the local Hamilton show. They would be paraded, heads bowed, half-naked, outside the boxing tent for all to view as strange specimens of humanity. The ringmaster would challenge the locals to 'show 'em how tough you are. Come on! See if you can knock out this fierce Abo! He once beat the best in Melbourne.' The scene was one of ugly exploitation; we believed that fighting an Aborigine was like fighting an animal, and winning was a sign of considerable prowess — and an achievement much sought after by local young people.

One of my saddest memories is of my father telling me how, as a youth of sixteen, he took up the challenge at the Hamilton show and beat several boxers in the ring. And, in my father's words, 'the last one was a big Abo'. My father won a medal for his efforts, but when his parents discovered his exploits, he was hauled before the Lutheran pastor and threatened with excommunication. His sin — not his racist attitude toward Aborigines in the troop, but participating in the 'public evil' of boxing!

Perhaps the most famous Aborigine to appear at the Hamilton show was Mulga Fred. He would put on a display of whipcracking that both amazed and amused the crowd until, by the end of the day, the grog would render him rather dangerous — especially when cracking a cigarette from between someone's lips. Mulga Fred is the Aboriginal man who appears on an infamous old advertisement for Pelaco shirts speaking the words 'Mine tinkit dey fit'. Sad to say, as a youth I saw nothing offensive in the advertisement or my own racist attitudes to Aboriginal people.

In my seminary training I recall no discussion of racism as a doctrine alongside the many church doctrines I learned. As immature seminarians, we firmly believed that black people, including Aborigines, had souls, but we still had an underlying belief that somehow they were uncivilised, heathen and intellectually inferior to us. We were deluded by our white education and our white history. Aborigines needed to be saved — but they also needed to be civilised. The poison of racism had penetrated our thoughts and our theology.

This insidious evil had so infiltrated our thinking that we viewed all Aborigines as unfortunate heathens belonging to a lesser 'race'. We did not know that the indigenous people of Adelaide were the Kaurna or that one community in the Barossa was Peramangk. We did not know their names or their history. We saw them as all the same — 'Aborigine' — and we relegated them all to the margins of our lives and our communities. They were the object of our mission programs and charitable acts that made us feel generous. They were not a civilised people like us, a people from whom we could learn about life, a people with a distinctive human identity. We taught them; they were expected to listen and learn — despite their allegedly limited IQ.

I only began to explore the nature of racism when I went to America in the late 1950s. I became involved in what was called 'race relations'. At first I assumed, like many members of the dominant culture, that racism was basically a matter of ignorance. I was informed by some of my teachers that if I knew about the culture of another 'race', I would understand them and my racism would disappear. How naive! Some of the most educated people I met — including anthropologists and fellow clergy — were fiercely racist. My racism was not based on ignorance.

Nor was my racism based on fear. Just the opposite: racism created my fear, fed on my fear, and perpetuated my fear. I still remember the apprehension I felt when I first arrived at the St Louis railway station in 1955 and called for a cab. The driver was a big black man — what the locals then called a 'nigger'. The as yet unnamed racist poison rose up within me and left me paralysed, wondering why I had ever left Australia and how I could be at the mercy of someone so totally different from myself. Later I saw God's humorous hand in that journey: the taxidriver dropped me off in front of a statue of the Virgin Mary at a Catholic College instead of a statue of Luther at the Lutheran Seminary.

A second solution to the vexing issue of racism was offered by liberal white preachers. They viewed racism as a form of prejudice. This particular prejudice, they said, is grounded in the natural tendency of all humans to think of themselves or their people as superior (ethnocentrism).

Others claimed racism was a natural extension of original sin — that is, the sin of self-centredness committed by our first parents. In other words, our first parents are to blame. Like other prejudices, racism — it was claimed — can be overcome by an educational process which transforms our psyche, our inner attitudes. The white liberals, with their souls apparently cleansed of racism, declared themselves one with the blacks.

I soon discovered, in the civil rights movements of the 1960s, that racism was not the same as prejudice. What I experienced is reflected in the words of the African educator Paulus Zulu.

> Liberals like to believe that white prejudice is the root cause of racism and that this prejudice grows out of fear and ignorance. Black people know that this is a terrible lie, which has the effect of mystifying racism. Racist prejudice, ignorance and fears don't just happen.
> They are set up by people who are not fools. What we deliberately hide from our children in schools constructs racist ignorance. The way the media draws 'race' into reports of violence shapes racist fears. Everything teaches us to target the manufactured prejudices against Black people ... Prejudice is more the product of racism than its cause. (Moore 1993, pp. 4–5)

In the civil rights movement it became clear that racism was the basis of social and political policies of many US bodies, including the government. Racism was a system of beliefs that grounded the way institutions, governments and communities ordered and controlled society. Racism was, in fact, an ideology, a way of looking at the world that was believed to be valid and true. Racism was an intellectual toxin administered by social, educational and political powers. And the church was not exempt.

When I began to lament how widely this ideology permeated American thinking and life, I was quietly told to go home and reflect on the White Australia Policy or Australia's policy excluding Aboriginal people from full citizenship in their own country. Did this same ideology, this same sin, permeate Australian history and society? Admittedly racism in Australia was not promoted to justify a slave trade; but the evils it perpetrated, I soon discovered, were just as inhuman and ugly. I was forced to read Australian history again.

I was not born a racist, but from my childhood I was unconsciously indoctrinated with racist beliefs. I ingested the virus of racism with my intellectual, political and religious food: these beliefs came with my education, with my religious heritage and with Australian politics. They were absorbed through the media messages in the 1950s. Racism is a learned belief — an ideology that I assumed was reality. It is a poison that blinds us to the way things are in the world. Until very recently, racism was part of my being Australian; perhaps a residue of this evil still remains in me.

The sin of racism

Why is racism such a formidable barrier to reconciliation? What is this poison and why is it so difficult to remove from the Australian system?

First, racism is the false belief that 'races' actually exist. According to this belief, human beings do not constitute one human race, but belong to distinct groups or races with identifiable physical, intellectual and biological differences. The dark skin, broad brow and crinkly hair of some Aboriginal Australians was proof, so my teachers said, that different races existed. For them — and for many people today — the existence of races is not questioned.

The second and perhaps the most insidious part of this doctrine is the belief that some 'races' are inferior to others intellectually, morally and culturally. Black races, it was asserted, did not possess the same intellect as the superior white races. Black races, moreover, were believed to be motivated by baser human instincts; white races were guided by higher and more rational ideals.

The third aspect of racism — one which makes it so credible — is the belief that the identification of races was grounded in science. This belief was not a pious tradition or something derived originally from the Bible, though some had found texts in the Bible to support the doctrine. Racism emerged as a belief which was grounded in the misguided sciences of the 18th and 19th centuries. For various reasons, virtually all Europeans imbibed that belief until it became an assumed truth. I, and my ancestors, are heirs of that assumed truth; we must now acknowledge that our beliefs were wrong, as was our behaviour based on these beliefs.

A fourth and fundamental feature of racism is its character as an ideology, a system of beliefs that was developed and appropriated not only by individuals but also, and more importantly, by the social and political institutions in countries such as America, South Africa and Australia. Racism is therefore a social force and a political doctrine. Within a racist society, individuals tend to accept the dominant ideology as true — the way things are. Racism has infiltrated the worldview of most Europeans. Like all ideology, it is considered to be 'the way things are'.

This ideology had become the justification for numerous economic and social programs. Leaving aside the slave trade in America, this ideology justified the acquisition of colonial lands around the globe. This ideology supported the great expansion of missions in 18th and 19th century and contributed to the power of England and her colonies. To reject it as wrong would have been seen as thankless and as a failure to recognise God's colonial blessings.

This insidious ideology was part of the accepted Eurocentric worldview of most of our ancestors. Racism is not simply one of many sins committed by our immigrant grandparents —as a primal force it came with the First Fleet and gave rise to a long list of injustices throughout Australian history. The sin of racism, therefore, must be exposed for what it is, and its credibility must be destroyed, if we are to achieve reconciliation.

Racism is an insidious ideology, not only because it masquerades as truth and science, but because it has the capacity to activate tendencies found in most human beings. Racism taps into a common human propensity to believe that 'my way is better than yours'. Racism feeds the ego of human beings who want to boost themselves at the expense of others. Racism justifies the greed of those who take advantage of the less fortunate. And racism feeds the fear that rises in many of us when we are confronted with people who are 'different' or 'other'.

Racism is not just another archaic belief from our past. Racism is a destructive ideology that has prevented us from even considering the question of reconciliation until recent years. Today, while most Australians may have a better understanding of this ideology, and the Australian government has passed *The Racial Discrimination Act 1975*, racism has not been eliminated from our social system. It has poisoned our souls. Racism remains a negative force which needs to be identified, exposed and overcome if non-indigenous Australians are to be reconciled with the indigenous peoples of this land.

The development of the concept of 'race'

Until the 18th century, the word 'race' was rarely used and seemed to refer to a group of things having something in common. So Robert Burns in 1786 speaks of 'the pudding race', meaning puddings as a category of food.

Linnaeus, in his writings in 1751, was apparently the first to use 'race' as a term to classify humans. He and other writers of that era began to use the term in a new and radical way to designate broad subspecies of humans who can be differentiated from each other as distinct races on *biological* grounds. This idea led biologists and anthropologists to search for those biological differences in human beings which would justify the concept of distinct 'racial types'. To justify and humanise their classifications they examined hair colour, skin pigmentation, nose and lip size, and especially the shape of the skull.

Interest in the concept of race was closely linked to the social and political developments of the late 18th and early 19th centuries, especially with the struggle to abolish the slave trade. Racism also provided an ideology which served the economic purposes of the colonial powers in the 19th and 20th centuries. It served to justify their conquest of new lands and their exploitation of human lives. African blacks were often classified as a race who were closer to apes than to humans, and therefore suitable for exploitation as slave labour.

The so-called 'science of race' enabled people to classify indigenous people in the colonies as inferior 'by nature' rather than simply by virtue of their ignorance about God. Such people were not only infidels; they were also inherently ignorant and intellectually deprived. This biological approach was already anticipated by philosophers such as David Hume and Immanuel Kant, who both held that 'negroes are naturally inferior to whites'. Kant, while recognising that humans were only one species, identified four races according to skin colour; each 'race' was associated with a particular climate.

> First race: very blond (Northern Europe), of damp
> cold.
> Second race: copper-red (America), of dry cold.
> Third race: black (Senegambia), of dry heat.
> Fourth race: olive-yellow (Indians), of dry heat.
> (Eze 1997, p. 48)

A work which became an authoritative text on race toward the end of the 18th century was Johann Blumenbach's

On The Natural Varieties of Mankind. Blumenbach divided humanity into five races: Caucasian, Mongolian, Ethiopian, American, and Malay. He advocated a theory of degeneration of all other races from the Caucasian race which he described as the most beautiful race of men [sic], with rosy cheeks, oval faces, narrow noses, subglobular heads, perpendicular teeth and so on! (Eze 1997, pp. 79–90). Neither scientists nor philosophers could agree, however, on a single classification for the 'races' of humanity. By the end of the century, when Captain Cook was first encountering the Aboriginal peoples of Australia, the American edition of the *Encyclopaedia Britannica*, under the entry *Negro: Homo pelli nigri*, reflects a widely accepted view of the 'negro race' that persisted until well into this century — and in some circles still persists today.

> A name given to a variety of human species, who are entirely black and are found in the torrid zone ... round cheeks, high cheek bones, a forehead somewhat elevated, a short, broad, flat nose, thick lips, small ears, ugliness, and irregularity of shape, characterise their external appearance. The negro women have their loins greatly depressed, and very large buttocks, which give the back the shape of a saddle. Vices the most notorious seem to be the portion of this unhappy race: idleness, treachery, revenge, cruelty, impudence, stealing, lying, profanity, debauchery, nastiness and intemperance, are said to have extinguished the principles of natural law, and have silenced the reproofs of conscience. They are strangers to every sentiment of compassion and are an awful example of the corruption of man when left to himself. (Eze 1997, pp. 93–4)

The so-called 'Negro' race, then, was viewed as the epitome of corruption and living evidence of how the natural depravity of humans may even expunge the natural law — or in the language of St Paul — the law of God written in the human heart (Romans 2:14).

With the advent of Charles Darwin in the middle of the 19th century, the racism debate took another turn. No longer were humans considered the descendants of a common source like Adam; they were considered the pinnacle of a process of evolution from simpler forms of life. Different species emerged by a process of struggle with — and adaptation to — the environment. The final stage of evolution, according to Darwinian theory, is the progression from apes to *homo erectus* and *homo sapiens*.

Darwin accepted the existence of races, but did not view the recognised marks of skin colour, eye shape and skull morphology as evidence of the superiority of one race over another. Rather, he argued for a process of selection by sexual propensities. Selective breeding resulted from choosing preferred physical characteristics such as skin colour or eye shape; this choice also corresponded to geographic domains.

Cultural Darwinism, which developed from Darwin's ideas but was not part of his original theory, interpreted the struggle of species for survival as evidence of culturally superior races destined to dominate, and inferior races destined for extinction. Interbreeding with races lower on the ladder was thought to be threatening; it could lead to the degeneration of races higher on the ladder. By the beginning of the 20th century, Cultural Darwinism provided the grounds for the idea of a hierarchy of races (Stepan 1982, p. 55). The development of the concept of race is summarised by McConnochie, Hollinsworth and Pettman.

> Over a period of some 200 years, then, the idea of race was progressively refined by western society, from initially being simply a term for a group of people with something in common with one another, to being a concept which was used to explain human culture, and cultural inferiority and superiority, as the necessary consequences of biological differences between separate

subgroupings of the human species. It is a concept
which has been used to justify oppression, to deny
human rights (and indeed humanity) to millions of
people, and to direct the attempted or actual genocide
of millions of people. It is a concept which still has
immense power to generate hatred and oppression and
to produce intense hatred in people, whether they are
the perpetrators or victims of racism. (McConnochie,
Hollinsworth & Pettman 1989, p. 15)

Since the 1950s most scholars reject the belief that clear-
cut differences between so-called 'races' can be determined
on biological grounds. All human beings have the vast
majority of genetic materials in common. 'The distribution of
genetic codes is such that there is enormous variability within
groups thought of as different "races"' (Hollinsworth 1998,
p. 30). Population movements over thousands of years and
the consequent mixing of peoples means that 'there never
were "pure races" which were composed of people with
identical chromosomes' (Hollinsworth 1998, p. 30).

Race, then, has no biological reality independent of the
beliefs of the observer. Rather, race is a social construction, a
modern collective invention. As a social construct, race is a
living concept in contemporary society and persists in media
reports, school texts and government legislation. The precise
meaning of this concept in popular usage is quite fluid,
depending on the social and political context and the relative
power of those using the term. The specific 'races' that most
speakers have in mind when they use this term today remain
obscure, and they are hard-pressed, when challenged, to
identify the so-called 'races of humanity'. In popular parlance
within the Australian context, the term 'race' seems to be used
to distinguish between 'white Australians', 'Aborigines' and
'Asians'. The assumption in that classification is that 'white
Australians' are racially different and superior, though some
users of the term refute that assumption.

Racism and the church

'Race' in the precise sense of the term defined above does not occur in the Bible. There are no discrete 'races' identified by biological or physical characteristics. Rather, the Scriptures speak of countries, nations, and peoples. The story of the tower of Babel makes it quite explicit that the human race is classified in terms of culture, or more specifically, language — the bearer of culture (Genesis 11:1–9). The human groups who scatter across the earth are identified, first and foremost, by their languages.

The preceding chapter of Genesis outlines the descendants of Shem with a more detailed classification 'according to their families, their languages, their lands and their nations' (Genesis 10:32). These classifications are used throughout the Bible to identify peoples in a descriptive way that does not include the intellectual, biological or cultural superiority implied in the term 'race'. Even the concept of 'holy seed' is not grounded in race ideology, but is apparently designed to keep the Jewish line free from the religious pollution of aliens (Ezra 9).

Race ideology became such a consuming force in America during the 18th and 19th century that some Christians involved in the slave trade turned to the Bible to justify their actions. Racist readers found grounds for their beliefs in the story of Ham's drunkenness in Genesis 9. Ham, who 'saw the nakedness of his father Noah', is seen as the culprit. His sin, it is argued, led to a curse on his descendants in Africa. Among those descendants, given in the following chapter, are listed the Cushites (Ethiopians), one of the black peoples of Africa. As cursed peoples, it was assumed, the blacks could be enslaved as the inevitable outcome of their condemnation as children of Ham.

A close look at the text reveals, in fact, that Ham is not cursed at all. The curse is passed on to the next generation: to Canaan the son of Ham. The relevant passage reads,

'Cursed be Canaan, lowest of the slaves shall he be to his brothers' (Genesis 9:25). This curse, however, has nothing to do with the physical appearance of these people, their intellect or their culture. It simply declares that the Canaanites will experience the social status of being slaves to other peoples. This curse, it would seem, provides additional justification for Joshua's conquest and enslavement of the Canaanites for the Israelite reader.

In a fascinating book entitled *The Apartheid Bible*, Bobby Loubser traces how the Scriptures were read by South African whites in terms of their racist beliefs. The so-called 'theory of Ham', based on the text of Genesis discussed above, influenced popular theology and thinking from the early 18th to the beginning of the 20th century. Even after the abolition of slavery, the national consciousness of the whites in the 19th century was dominated by the principle of 'no equality'. 'No equality' was described as 'no marriages between blacks and whites, no blacks in church, no equality before the law and no compassion for their situation' (Loubser 1987, p. 14).

The Dutch Reformed Church of South Africa supported the policy of segregation and racial superiority, turning to the Scriptures to justify its stance against unity and equality.

> From all this Totius deduced two principles: 'Firstly, that which God has joined together no man should put asunder. This is the essence of the plea for the unity of the (Afrikaner) people ... Secondly, we may not join together that which God has separated. In pluriformity the council of God is realised. The higher unity in Christ is of a spiritual nature. Therefore *no equality* and no miscegenation', because equality is directly against the great principle of God's order at the Tower of Babel. (Loubser 1987, p. 57)

These so-called theological principles translated into national, social and religious apartheid. The use of the Bible to justify racist beliefs and separatist practices is also found in Australia. It was common in the 19th century to regard the Aboriginal people as the 'ultimate example of the curse of Ham', as John Harris demonstrates.

> Were the Aborigines, asked William Hull in 1846, 'degraded descendants of the nations driven out by divine command to the uttermost parts of the earth and the islands of the seas?' It was not simply that 'like the Hittites and the Jebusites and the Aboriginal Canaanites, they have been left to the natural consequences of the effects of not retaining the knowledge of God', but that of all peoples in that condition, the Aborigines were judged to be on 'the lowest scale of degraded humanity'. To the Wesleyan clergyman, Joseph Orton, the Aborigines were degraded 'far below the brute creation'. (Harris 1990, p. 30)

In spite of widespread acceptance of the belief that Australian Aborigines were also descended from the cursed family of Ham, many early missionaries saw all people, no matter how depraved, as being children of Adam and therefore, in some sense, fellow human beings with souls. Though missionary Schulz at Hermannsburg considered indigenous Australians 'degenerate, living like animals, naked, eating distasteful things and sleeping in the open' (Harris 1990, p 392), he and others believed that they could be educated.

> The Aborigines are not unable to be educated ... It makes me cross to read or hear degrading judgement about these people. They have sunk deep spiritually indeed for in spite of all our efforts we have found no trace of any religious act among them. Nevertheless, they are Adam's children, the first glance indicates it. With their beautiful slender bodies six feet tall, as well as the capabilities of mind, in many respects they even excel Christians. (Harris 1990, p. 392)

In the light of these attitudes within the church, Anne Pattel-Gray speaks not only of institutional racism where the structure and policies of an organisation are racist; she also speaks of 'Christian racism', and traces the history of racism as a 'heresy' and 'theological error' in the church. Especially significant is her claim that the Australian churches still contribute to racism in Australia. She cites Don Dunstan as saying that 'to pass a resolution and make a public statement' of apology is not enough. The church should be actively involved in fighting for the rights of Aboriginal peoples (Pattel-Gray 1998, p. 148). She claims that the Uniting Church apologised for the actions of its Presbyterian ancestors, but it completely failed to address the issue of compensation for its past injustices, and for its present and future benefiting from (exploitation of) such injustices. (Some would dispute this claim in the light of recent resolutions by bodies such as the Victorian Synod of the Uniting Church.) Other denominations, too, have condemned racism, but not implemented a serious anti-racism policy within the church. Still others have ignored both the heresy of racism, and the history of injustices perpetrated as a result of racism — they see neither as fundamental to the study of theology in Australia. Implicit racism persists in many of the policies and practices of churches in Australia.

Racism is not simply a sin committed by racist individuals but a poison which has infected the whole fabric of Australian society, its institutions and world view. Racism is part of the suppressed side of who we are as Australians. Racism was an established belief among the first European settlers and most, if not all, of the many immigrants who followed them. Racism is a corporate evil, a structural sin, a social belief. It is the primal sin of the Europeans who invaded this land, a sin that gave rise to the numerous crimes of dispossession, desecration and destruction perpetrated against the indigenous peoples of Australia (Byrne 1992, p. 66).

The effects of racism

The tragic story of racism in Australia has been treated in detail in a number of recognised works (Hollinsworth, 1998; Pattel-Gray, 1998). Rather than recount this record, I will emphasise some of the major effects of racism that immigrant Australians must address if they are to pursue authentic reconciliation. In the previous chapter I identified seven sins, among others, perpetrated against indigenous Australians: dispossession, genocide, dehumanisation, destruction of culture, massacre, desecration, assimilation. All of these sins have their origin in the primal sin of racism that conditioned immigrant Australians to treat fellow human beings as 'brutes'. I shall discuss the connection between racism and the loss of land from the Aboriginal people, the crushing of living Aboriginal cultures, and the process of dehumanisation.

Loss of land: dispossession

The very act of Britain claiming sovereignty over Australia and the subsequent legal fiction of *terra nullius* were grounded in the pervasive racist ideology. The racist frontier mentality of most early settlers justified the clearing of Aboriginal peoples together with the clearing of the trees and wildlife. Racism was more than an attitude: it provided a charter for cutting off Aboriginal inhabitants from their home, their country, their 'mother'. Racist beliefs enabled settlers to clear their consciences when they dispossessed, displaced and exterminated Aboriginal peoples.

> The 1830s and 1840s saw the rapid expansion of the frontier and with the establishment of the colonies of Victoria, Western Australia and South Australia, the issue of Aboriginal policies and practices reached crisis point. To the vast majority of settlers the Aborigines were simply an impediment to taking up the land. They were considered as part of the fauna and flora, like

dingoes and emus — something to be cleared from the land to allow farming and grazing to develop in a safe, tidy and profitable environment. (McConnochie, Hollinsworth & Pettman 1989, p. 58)

While a few concerned philanthropists and clergy, such as Pastor Kavel in South Australia (Reynolds 1992, p. 137), sought to provide reserves for dispossessed Aboriginal communities, few had any inkling of the trauma, physical and spiritual pain caused by separating these indigenous Australians from their land. As Reynolds points out, the efforts of these concerned citizens was futile in the face of the ideology of racism.

The philanthropic individuals who took up the Aboriginal cause were well aware that they were swimming against the tide and that fellow colonists held them in contempt. They appreciated too that the conflict over ideas grew out of and was shaped by the struggle over land, that racism was as functional for the frontier squatter as the Colt revolver. One cleared the land, the other cleared the conscience. (Reynolds 1996, p. 104)

For many Aboriginal people, the wounds caused by being severed from their land — even 200 years ago — have never been healed. With the loss of land came loss of identity, loss of connection with the spiritual domain, and loss of place in the world. The two hundred years of suffering caused by this enduring injustice is due ultimately to the sin of racism. The wounds from these injustices still need to be healed as part of the reconciliation process.

Loss of culture: demonisation

It is doubtful whether the racist British administration would have even used the term 'culture' in relation to Aboriginal life. As Harris points out, Aboriginal culture was beyond the comprehension of the early settlers.

Most of the more thoughtful settlers were satisfied to
accept that in the 'chain of being' Aboriginal people
occupied a place a little above the animals, if at all. The
view of the clergy was in practice only slightly more
enlightened. Aborigines were degraded descendants of
Ham, almost removed from the reach of the Gospel.
(Harris 1990, pp. 43–44)

The racist policies of Australia in the early years operated
with the expectation either that the Aboriginal 'race' would
eventually die out, or, if not, these so-called 'savages' would
need to be 'civilised' and live like their European masters.
For this 'civilising' process to happen, the indigenous
inhabitants were expected to reject their traditional ways and
become 'whites'. Ultimately their traditional culture was to
be crushed — 'for their own good'.

Early missionaries — except for a few cases where they
learned the local native tongue — resolutely demanded that
indigenous Australians give up their lifestyle and make a
complete break with their culture, a culture often viewed as
demonic. By 'demonising' Aboriginal culture, missionaries
made removal of its essentials into a form of exorcism.

Nineteenth century Christian missionaries generally
had two main aims: the conversion of the heathen to
Christianity and the introduction of European
'civilisation'. The process of civilising involved both
teaching the skills that would enable the people to fit into
European society, and convincing them to give up their
culture. The 'Christianising' and 'civilising' aims were
often mentioned together, as if they were inseparable.
Indeed, to the missionaries they were inseparable — to
them the rejection of pagan ways was as important as the
rejection of pagan religion. (Harris 1990, p. 72)

This racist belief that Aboriginal culture was base and
degraded was given additional force by many missionaries

who attributed this baseness to the work of the devil. Instead of seeing European culture as grounded in a racist lie, they saw Aboriginal culture as evidence of the 'father of lies'. As missionary Poland writes, those

> who try to reduce the status of Aborigines to the level of animals, and proceed to treat them accordingly, do them a terrible injustice. But it is also foolish to regard them as being better than they are or can be. Satan has them in his power. It follows that a spirit of deception must dominate their lives. (Poland 1988, p. 104)

Loss of humanity: dehumanisation

Racist descriptions of Aborigines as animals, savages or degraded specimens of humanity have been cited above. The tragic effect of treating indigenous Australians in this way meant that by the middle of this century most of those Aboriginal people who survived — and many thousands did not — were demoralised. Generations of humiliation meant that many had internalised the very idea of inferiority promoted by the racist ideology. Few appreciated the rights they possessed as human beings. The force of this demoralisation is summarised by Aboriginal activist Paul Coe.

> They have been forced to forego much of their self-respect. All this 'metho' drinking is the manifestation of a cause: the alienation of the people from the land, the alienation of the people from their own culture, people denied any right to decide their own future, denied the basic powers every white man [sic] takes for granted in this country. This is the right to bring up kids the way you want to bring them up ... For the last fifty years this has screwed up just about every black in this country. It is going to take about ten or twenty years to overcome the effects of this because the effects are so deeply ingrained in the kids, this kind of inferiority attitude that before you do anything you must ask the

white man [*sic*] for it, you must ask permission. (Tatz
& McConnochie 1975, p. 104)

The inhuman practice of taking children from their
Aboriginal parents — ostensibly for their own good — and
placing them in so-called orphanages, such as Colebrook
Home in Adelaide, enabled such institutions to 'brainwash'
its inmates with the doctrine of racism. Ironically, many of
the people who were treated so poorly are now leading the
resistance against racism, and demanding the establishment
of human rights for all Aboriginal peoples.

The poison in our soul

Whenever most of us make connection with Australia's
heritage, we tend to make that connection with moments in
the immigrant history of Australia. Few of us would point to
the attempted genocide in Tasmania or the misery of
Maralinga as evidence of our Australian identity. The tragic
reality is that much of our history has a hidden side that is
both justified and suppressed by racism. From the arrival of
the First Fleet, key features of our history have been
characterised by racism.

It is naive to believe that racism is dead in Australia and
that this challenge is past. In some contexts it may be dormant
and relatively private. In other cases it may be the implicit
practice behind a public policy of equity. The poison can,
however, easily be revived. Even if the term 'race' is used less
precisely today than in previous generations, the term still has
the power to activate the racism deep within us. The rhetoric
of the One Nation Party, for example, activated dormant racist
attitudes in parts of Australia. I experienced these attitudes
again recently when a tradesman was laying some carpet in my
house. In the course of the conversation 'race' was mentioned.
'What is the best Aborigine?' he asked. Foolishly I humoured
him and said, 'I don't know'. 'A dead one', he replied.

It is hard to avoid the conclusion that our soul as Australians has been poisoned by this pervasive evil. Wherever I search in our history, I discover this racism and the benefits that immigrant Australians have derived from racist policies. European Australians have been 'blessed' through the power of racism. This land is not a clean gift from God, but a treasure stolen in the name of racism.

If we are to expunge this poison from our system, we need more than individual confessions. This infection has permeated the political, social and religious institutions and beliefs of our society. The sin is corporate. The cure requires more than a few cosmetic changes, more than a political 'treaty' in the year 2001. The process of reconciliation demands isolating this poison, telling both sides of our history boldly — preferably in the media for all to hear — confessing our crimes in rites of healing, implementing an anti-race campaign more intense than any anti-smoking campaign, and making education 'all Australian' rather than 'white Australian'. The anti-venom required is probably an intense probing of the individual and collective soul as we each confront the poison within.

It is important to remember in this search that the Australian soul or spirit is not a European soul in the process of being acclimatised to a harsh new environment. The Australian soul emerges from our land, our collective history, our people. And that heritage embraces both indigenous and non-indigenous Australians. The racism that has infected us, therefore, involves also the indigenous peoples. They have been forced to imbibe our poisoned values. As I seek to grasp our collective identity as Australians, it is impossible for me to imagine what it must have been like to suffer the endless ignominy of being told I was 'a worthless Abo', 'a savage', 'a pathetic creature', 'a lazy dog'. I can hardly begin to comprehend what it was like to be humiliated, ridiculed and abused as an inferior being for years and years. It is hard even to speak about the molesting of children, the poisoning of rations and the raping of women. Yet, this is part of our collective history. It is part of who we are as Australians.

If there is to be authentic reconciliation, then, as Anne Pattel-Gray rightly says, immigrant Australians must repent of the primal sin of racism and change their whole attitude to indigenous Australians. Without purging the poison, it will continue to condition those in power to be racist. The efforts of the various institutions concerned with reconciliation will be futile if they 'continue to focus on the symptoms of injustice and never on the sources of injustice' (Pattel-Gray 1998, p. 239).

CHAPTER 5

BEFORE THE EUROPEANS
ARRIVED

When we talk of God — and the old fellas know — God
is not the Whitefella way, up above here. God is here with
me. That's the way it is. God's not just grounded, hiding
behind the butt of that tree. The presence of the Creator is
there in the tree, in the land, in each one of us. You don't
need to do a Pentecostal-type service, right? You don't
need to carry out all sorts of observances. You just need to
communicate with the Creator. And that Creator's always
been with Aboriginal people. (Gilbert 1996, p. 62)

*In this chapter I consider the principle of identity (outlined in
chapter 2) as it relates to Aboriginal culture and Aboriginal
spirituality in particular. I explore the difficulty of valuing a
culture that immigrant Australians have, in the past, devalued.
I cite the story of Abraham and Melchizedek as a biblical
precedent for affirming both the culture and the God of the
land to which Abraham and Sarah immigrate. In exploring
possible connections between my understanding of the Spirit*

and Aboriginal spirituality, I explore the 'Spirit of the Land' and the 'Law' as experienced by Aboriginal peoples.

Devaluing culture

I grew up in two cocoons, two subcultures. The first was a small farming community that protected itself against the rest of society by valuing a practical mateship view of the world, and suspected intellectuals or upper-class people as being dangerous 'tall poppies'. The second was a tightly controlled Lutheran community that guarded itself against possible heretical influences by avoiding marriage, worship or serious dialogue with people of other faiths. In both communities, the 'other' outside my cocoons threatened me and my familiar world. Any attempt to understand the 'other' or 'other cultures' was considered folly. The day I suggested that I might go to high school rather than finish my schooling at the local one-room primary school and then work on the farm, my father said, 'You're bloody mad!' When I persisted he replied, 'Well, you can ride your bike all ten miles to town. And don't ask for any sympathy.' When I hinted later that I might go on to university or seminary, my father simply replied, 'Now I know you are mad.' The intellectual world was 'other', threatening, the domain of 'know-alls' who 'thought they were superior' to less-educated farmers.

A measure of confidence and assurance is needed for people to leave their cocoons and seek to understand the culture of 'the other', whoever the other may be. Church leaders hammered into me that I should never worship with people of other denominations; if I did I would fail to stand up for the truth I was confessing in my own denomination. The suggestion that I might be open to the culture of an Aboriginal community — except to learn ways that the church might communicate the Gospel more effectively — was even more unthinkable. In the reconciliation process today, however, non-indigenous Australians are asked to 'recognise indigenous cultures as a valued part of our Australian heritage'. This task may prove difficult, not only because indigenous cultures have been 'other' and 'alien' for many people, but also because Aboriginal cultures have been so vigorously devalued in the past. Non-indigenous Australians are now being asked to value cultures that many of their ancestors previously rejected as pagan.

Until recently, racist beliefs caused most non-indigenous Australians to view Aboriginal cultures as worthless and heathen. Aboriginal cultures were considered 'depraved' expressions of human development when compared with the 'civilised' cultures of the Western world. Government policy demanded, therefore, that Aborigines become 'civilised' or disappear. Their cultures were thought to have no intrinsic value.

In contrast, early anthropologists were fascinated by Aboriginal cultures — their rituals, beliefs and spirituality. Indigenous Australians became a living specimen of 'stone-age culture'. They were classified as tribal, primitive or primal, thereby differentiating them from more 'advanced societies'. Famous scholars, such as Mircea Eliade, wrote extensively about Australian Aborigines as 'primitives' without ever visiting the country.

Again, going against the trend, some anthropologists, such as Ted Strehlow, lived from their youth among a particular indigenous community, mastered the language and provided sympathetic portraits of Aboriginal life. According to Strehlow,

[a] study of Australian Aboriginal beliefs presents many problems. One of these arises from the attitudes of the European observer which are always apt to colour his observations. As Professor Stanner has expressed it, the older anthropological writers who described the beliefs of the Aboriginal population were baffled to find

among the Australian tribes a religion without God, without any creeds or church or priests, without any concern for 'sin' or sexual morals (in the European sense), and without any 'material show'. Yet modern anthropologists are undoubtedly correct in stating that each Australian Aboriginal group religion 'is a living faith, something quite inseparable from the pattern of everyday life and thought'. (Strehlow 1977, p. 4)

Given this heritage, it may be difficult for some Australians to value what they once denounced as pagan and worthless. It is hard to face the ugly stories of our common history about the many atrocities and injustices perpetrated by European immigrants in the name of 'civilisation'. It may be even harder to acknowledge publicly that I — like so many others — was very wrong about Aboriginal culture.

In recent years, non-indigenous Australians have begun to value some features of Aboriginal cultures in the fields of art, performance and music. The incorporation of Aboriginal Studies into university and school courses has led to a limited study of Aboriginal beliefs and customs. I suggest that in most schools, however, while the study of stories, arts, crafts and customs have been incorporated into the curriculum, there has not been a corresponding interest in developing an appreciation of spirituality and the sacred in Aboriginal cultures. It is my belief that when the spiritual and the sacred are removed from an appreciation of cultures, a new form of devaluing occurs.

The task ahead, if I am to be true to the reconciliation process, is to break out of both my cultural cocoons and search Aboriginal culture for more than boomerangs and didgeridoos. I need to set aside my cultural arrogance and listen to the sounds of the Aboriginal spirituality that is also part of my Australian heritage. In that search I may find that the vital songs in Australia's soul can be discerned in the period before the Europeans came.

A biblical precedent

First let me outline a biblical precedent which illustrates how Abraham and Sarah discovered the God of the land, the indigenous Creator God of Canaan, and affirmed that deity as their own. The Abraham–Sarah cycle of stories portrays Abraham, Sarah and their family household as a community at peace with their new host country, Canaan (Habel 1995, chapter 7).

On one occasion Abraham and Sarah are confronted by a crisis (Genesis 14). A coalition of four kings from the east had invaded the land, captured the city of Sodom and taken its inhabitants captive. Abraham's nephew, Lot, and his family, are among the booty. Abraham immediately gathers a small army of 318 men from their extended household and sets off in pursuit to rescue all the captives including their relatives. Abraham is successful and returns with everything, including 'his nephew Lot, his goods, the women and the people' intact.

On his way home Abraham, and all the former captives visit the sacred site of Salem. The kings of Salem and Sodom roll out the red carpet. Abraham has won the friendship of two important Canaanite communities. The Canaanite leaders of these communities do not ask Abraham for the name of the deity who enabled him to achieve this feat. They do not treat Abraham as a stranger who worships a foreign god. Instead they share food and wine together, an action which celebrates genuine fellowship between them.

Melchizedek, the indigenous priest of Salem, then blesses Abraham in the name of El Elyon — the God of the land, the Creator God of Canaan. Abraham responds by giving a tithe of 'everything,' thereby acknowledging El Elyon as the source of his achievements and Melchizedek as the legitimate indigenous priest of this shrine. Abraham and the two kings worship the same deity at the shrine of the indigenous people of the land. Abraham thereby recognises the indigenous God of the land as his own God, and the god of Sarah and his family group.

What is remarkable in this context is that the memory of Israel did not erase the fact that Abraham and Sarah, the first immigrants into Canaan recorded in the Hebrew Scriptures, worshipped El as the host deity of the land who welcomed them through an indigenous priest. The deity who called Abraham to leave Abraham's father in Haran and come to Canaan turns out to be the indigenous El, the Creator God of Canaan. Abraham and Sarah leave the gods of Babylon behind (Joshua 24.2) and recognise the indigenous deity as their own.

The precedent of Abraham and Sarah recognising the God of the land and Abraham respecting an indigenous priest of Canaan provides a biblical alternative to the way immigrating Europeans treated the indigenous people of Australia and their cultures. These immigrants did not ask about the God of the land, the Spirit in the land, the sacred sites of the land, or the spiritual beliefs in the land.

Is it too late to ask the question now? Who is the God of the land? What was the spirituality of Australia before Europeans arrived? How was the Creator experienced in traditional Aboriginal cultures? Does that same Spirit connect Aboriginal — and non-Aboriginal — people today?

In doing this, I am not seeking to romanticise Aboriginal beliefs and culture as if they will provide all the answers to Australia's spiritual search for meaning. Nor am I seeking to spurn my own spiritual heritage. Rather, my goal is, first, to value Aboriginal cultures as spiritual cultures in their own right, and second, to learn from their spiritual heritage and thereby enrich my own. In time this Aboriginal heritage may be recognised as part of a common Australian heritage, representing our deep spiritual roots in this land.

Valuing Aboriginal culture

Valuing culture is far more than appreciating those Aboriginal art, craft and dance forms which are now widely known, and have been transformed into so-called 'cultural industries' (Council 1994b, p. 13). In the context of the current reconciliation process, I contend that valuing Aboriginal cultures also means valuing the sacred and ethical dimensions of these cultures. It means respecting Aboriginal experiences of the spiritual as having intrinsic value, before seeking to make connections between these experiences of the Spirit and those reflected in another culture. I follow the lead of Galarrwuy Yunupingu and use the term 'Spirit' as shorthand for the 'spiritual world' of Aboriginal culture (Yunupingu 1996, p. 4). The following summarises how he experiences that Spirit today.

> As I travel around Australia I meet great leaders of Aboriginal and non-Aboriginal people. We talk about different things, but it all boils down to this Spirit that cannot be seen. It is like air; we breathe out of it, we live in it, but we do not feel it, we do not touch it. It is there; like I am standing here. The Ancestors of the land are standing with us. That Spirit is still strong all the time. (Yunupingu 1996, p. 9)

Non-indigenous Australians also use the term Spirit, often with specific reference to the Holy Spirit of Christianity. In this chapter, however, I am seeking, first of all, an empathetic understanding of the indigenous experience of the Spirit. I could designate the Spirit, as experienced by indigenous Australians and reflected in their culture, in a number of ways: coin a term such as 'Indigenous Spirit', adopt the title 'Creator Spirit' employed by the Rainbow Spirit Elders, or follow the cue of Yunupingu and use the expression 'Spirit of the Land' (Yunupingu 1996, p. 10). I have chosen to use 'Spirit of the Land' as a distinctive expression where 'Land' is capitalised as part of the title. In this chapter, Spirit may be used as shorthand for 'Spirit of the Land'.

I use the title 'Spirit of the Land' for several reasons. First, I believe it values Aboriginal culture and avoids a simplistic identification with Christian terms such as Holy

Spirit or Creator. Second, this designation recognises the distinctive and 'other' dimensions of Aboriginal experiences of the Spirit which are not mine. Aboriginal spirituality is land-oriented while much Western Christianity is heaven-oriented. In seeking to value and comprehend Aboriginal culture as an integral part of 'our common Australian heritage', I will seek points of connection with Aboriginal spirituality while affirming the distinctive 'otherness' of Aboriginal experiences of the spiritual.

The Spirit of the Land

Under this heading, I shall first focus on the profound spiritual dimension of Aboriginal culture. Given the widespread use of the term 'Dreaming' as shorthand for the spiritual core of Aboriginal culture, it is tempting to follow popular usage and employ this expression as a point of departure. Swain traces the origins of the term 'Dreaming' to a rendering of certain Aranda words meaning 'eternal/uncreated' and concludes that, in

> several Desert languages there is a linguistic connection between the 'self-derived eternal' and dreams, but this is not a universal occurrence. The word 'Dreaming' or 'Dream Time' has, nonetheless, returned from academic coinage through popular culture to spread throughout virtually all Aboriginal English speech: a self-fulfilling academic prophecy which began with a concept of which the Aboriginal linguist Eve Fesl says, 'Dreaming' is a compound word 'dreamed up' by an English speaker who couldn't understand Aboriginal languages. (Swain 1993, p. 21)

Djiniyini Gondarra states that he would prefer to avoid 'the Dreaming' — a term 'dreamed up' by anthropologists — and focus on the specifics of each culture. A recent text entitled *Rainbow Spirit Theology* also seeks to avoid the term because 'it seems to refer to something vague and dreamlike, something that is not real' (Rainbow Spirit Elders 1997, p. xi). What both parties passionately maintain, however, is that in Aboriginal culture there is an awareness of an eternal, profound, mysterious, spiritual reality that has always existed, and continues to exist, in Australia. That reality was present in the beginning, creating the landscape and the seascape and can best be expressed as the Spirit, or Spirit of the Land. This spiritual essence is still present deep within the landscape, especially in the sacred sites across the land and it is experienced in the sacred rituals, sacred stories and sacred symbols of the Aboriginal peoples.

According to the Rainbow Spirit Elders, the Spirit of the Land is the 'Creator Spirit' and is known by a variety of names, including the Rainbow Snake. The Spirit of the Land is experienced as a life-giving presence below the earth who causes life-forces to emerge from land and sea. The Spirit of the Land is the energising force present in sacred rites, sacred sites and sacred stories. When these sacred stories are told and the rites performed at specified sacred sites, the power of this Spirit is activated.

The indigenous experience of the Spirit of the Land is linked with plants, animals and individual human spirits in particular places. As Pat Dodson says, the

> land is a living place made up of sky, cloud, river,
> trees, the sand; and the Spirit has planted my own spirit
> there in my own country. It is something — and yet it is
> not a thing — it is a living entity. It belongs to me, I
> belong to it. I rest in it. I come from there. (Dodson
> 1993, p. 20)

It is not possible to discuss the numerous domains where experience of the Spirit of the Land is central to Aboriginal culture. One area that deserves special consideration, however, is sacred story, sometimes called 'Dreaming story'. This domain will serve to illustrate how I believe Aboriginal culture can be revalued.

There are at least four ways in which the stories, symbols and sites associated with Aboriginal experiences of the Spirit of the Land have been interpreted. The first is to view these 'alleged experiences' as the delusions of a primitive people, and merely fascinating expressions of the human imagination. Since the time of the European invasion, these stories have been collected to satisfy Western curiosity. There are numerous volumes of so-called Aboriginal legends in most Australian libraries. Most of these versions, alas, are written as simplified narratives and show little appreciation of the spiritual depth of the original story cycle. The presence of the Spirit of the Land in the formation of these stories is ignored. Given the widespread view that Aboriginal culture was primitive, these sacred stories were easily relegated to the category of folk tales. I recall once entering a classroom where the teacher was discussing 'Dreaming stories'. The children were asked to create a story with a title such as, 'Why do Kangaroos hop?' 'How did the echidna get her spikes?' 'Why doesn't the emu fly?' Clearly, Rudyard Kipling's 'just-so' stories provided the model for the teacher. There was no indication that these stories are the collective sacred memories of Aboriginal communities about spiritual things, believed to be filled with power, and handed down from the ancestors. Aboriginal culture is not valued as spiritual when sacred stories are treated as exotic tales designed to entertain children.

A second way of understanding these stories in educational contexts is to study them as typical phenomena of a discrete religion. Sacred creation stories can be analysed closely and compared with creation myths from other religions. Using this approach each component of Aboriginal religion — from sacred symbols to sacred stories — can be studied empathetically and compared with related phenomena in other religious systems. A model designed to enable high school students to study Aboriginal religion and culture according to this approach is found in the highschool text,

Finding a Way: Religious Worlds of Today. This approach is academic and appropriate in some contexts. I now find, however, it also keeps me too detached, and hinders me from trying to make connections with Aboriginal experiences of the Spirit of the Land. Nor do I have to value these experiences as having any importance in my search for the Australian soul. If no connection can be made between the two cultures at a spiritual level, then the Aboriginal people remain separate as indigenous, the Europeans immigrants remain immigrants, and the two cultures do not become part of our common heritage as Australians.

A third approach is to make a simple equation between creator beings, sacred rites, sacred symbols, and spiritual experiences in Aboriginal culture and those of Western Christianity. In this model, the argument then is that indigenous and non-indigenous Australians have experienced the same realities under different names. The danger is that this approach is a form of cultural appropriation incorporating indigenous rites and symbols into another religion as if they belonged to that religion. This approach ignores the distinctive indigenous experiences of the Spirit among Australian Aborigines, experiences that must be recognised as such if they are to be valued by all Australians.

The fourth approach, the one that I am attempting to follow in this study as more appropriate, is to acknowledge there are both powerful differences and possible connections between Aboriginal experiences of the Spirit of the Land and my Christian experiences of the Spirit of God, the Creator. The experiences of young people involved in an Aboriginal initiation rite at a sacred secret site will be very different from those of similarly aged young people being baptised in a Christian church. The one is an experience of the Spirit of the Land, perhaps as an ancestor being; the other is an experience of the Holy Spirit. Both experiences are respected as spiritual and significant in their respective cultures.

For me the 'otherness' I discern in Aboriginal experiences of the Spirit of the Land must be identified, not as a reason for rejecting them as pagan or heretical, but as grounds for understanding and valuing the work of the Spirit of the Land in ways beyond my limited cultural experience. A typical Aboriginal sacred story may depict an ancestor being emerging from the land or sea, transforming the landscape and returning into the land and sea. At various times this creator being may change from a human form into an animal form and vice versa. At first this seems very odd to those of us who grew up with the Genesis creation account, or with the story of evolution, as our guide to the mystery of our origins. I can, however, make particular connections between Aboriginal creation stories and Genesis 1 by pointing to passages dealing with the third and sixth days of creation, where flora and fauna (except humans) also 'emerge' from the earth. What is so 'other' for me about Aboriginal creation stories is that the creating powers themselves come from the earth and that these creating powers can be both human and animal — both sharing a common spirit that is expressed in two forms.

Is this experience of the Spirit of the Land therefore something I should reject? Far from it! The image of the Spirit as a celestial being who intervenes on earth as a divine being or spiritual presence may be part of my heritage. In an emerging Australian spirituality, the experience of the Spirit as the Spirit of the Land deep within creation may be just as significant. A spiritual kinship between humans, animals and the Spirit of the Land may be 'other' for me, but none the less lead me to a potential new understanding of the Spirit I already know.

This special connection or kinship between a human being and a particular species is sometimes referred to as 'totemism', a term derived from Native American contexts. This kinship may be with a living creature, such as a dingo, a bird, a honey ant or a fish. In some cases this kinship is with what we would call an inanimate object, such as a star. Whatever my 'totem' creature, or my personal 'dreaming', it has the same spirit as I do, and its spirit also resides along specific trails or at particular sites in the landscape. I relate to my 'totem' and 'dreaming' places in a special spiritual way. A custodian from the appropriate kinship group will be responsible for performing the ceremonies associated with my totem and preserving the sacred sites where my 'dreaming spirit' resides. I, in turn, may be a custodian responsible for the totemic species, sites and ceremonies of another group. Through these custodians, species are preserved, life is sustained, key relationships are maintained, and the land is kept sacred.

This spiritual kinship with other species and the environment seems to be at the heart of Aboriginal spirituality. According to Eddie Kneebone,

> Aboriginal spirituality is the belief and the feeling within yourself that allows you to become part of the whole environment — not the built environment, but the natural environment ... Birth, life and death are all part of it, and you welcome each. Aboriginal spirituality is the belief that all objects are living and share the same soul or spirit that Aboriginals share. Therefore all Aborigines have a kinship with the environment. The soul or spirit is common — only the shape of it is different, but no less important. (Mudrooroo 1995, pp. 33–4)

As a result of my own reconciliation journey, I now speak of a spiritual heritage that links me to this ancient land, a land where I was born. I too have a spiritual bond with this land. I now address the Spirit of the Land as a distinctive manifestation of the Spirit in a land common to indigenous and non-indigenous Australians. I now confess that the Creator Spirit I know was experienced as the Spirit of the Land in Australia long before Europeans arrived. Australia was not a godless land any more than Aboriginal culture was

BEFORE THE EUROPEANS ARRIVED

devoid of the Spirit. The Spirit of the Land was known in Australia long before Abraham and Sarah knew the God of the land in Canaan.

Indigenous Law

Many aspects of Aboriginal culture could have been selected to complement the preceding discussion of the Spirit of the Land. I have selected Law not only because it is central to Aboriginal society, but also because there seems to be a popular trend to explore Aboriginal culture primarily as spiritual and aesthetic, and to deny the relevance — or even existence — of substantial social, legal or other structures in Aboriginal culture. Valuing of Aboriginal Law is crucial to the reconciliation process. As Djiniyini Gondarra writes,

> I believe there can be no reconciliation in this country without the recognition of the Customary Law and systems of governance of the indigenous people of this land. (Gondarra 1998, p. 1)

Law in Aboriginal communities is more than a human code established by a governing body — it is Law spelled with a capital 'L'. While Law is variously described as coming from the ancestors, from the 'Dreaming' or from the ground, Law has always been. Law is believed to be eternal, unchanging, powerful, life-sustaining. Anthropologist Deborah Bird Rose quotes the words of Doug Campbell to demonstrate what Law means.

> You see that hill over there? Blackfellow Law like that hill. It never changes. Whitefellow law goes this way, that way, all the time changing. Blackfellow Law different. It never changes. Blackfellow Law hard — like a stone, like that hill. The Law is in the ground. (Rose 1992, p. 56)

The eternal unchanging character of Law among the Aranda is stressed by Paul Albrecht, a long-term missionary among this group of Aboriginal people. He emphasises that the Law is not dependent on memory, but is recorded in sacred objects (*tjurrunga*) in designated sacred sites. These *tjurrunga*, he maintains,

> play the same role in Aboriginal societies as constitutions do in our societies ... their constitutions cannot be changed or amended by men [*sic*], because they were given to men [*sic*] by the ancestral spirit beings. Hence they are eternal. (Albrecht 1998, p. 13)

According to Djiniyini Gondarra, the term for Law used among the Yolnju is *Madayin*; it embraces three governing principles:

> a) 'the law must create a state of peace, harmony and tranquillity, with true justice for all citizens';
> b) 'the law must be perfectly consistent with all the levels of law from the source to the minor acts of law';
> c) 'the law must be assented to by the citizens in a ceremony that shows that they are all under the discipline, responsibility and protection of the law'. (Gondarra 1998, pp. 1–2)

Just as significant as these principles, perhaps, are the social domains which this Law covered. According to Gondarra,

> *Madayin* includes: all the people's law, the instruments and objects that encode and symbolise the law, oral dictates, names and song cycles and the holy, restricted places that are used in the maintenance, education and development of law. The law covers the ownership of land and waters, the resources on or within these lands and waters, it regulates and controls; production and trade, the moral, social and religious law including laws for the conservation of, and the farming of, fauna, flora and aquatic life. (Gondarra 1998, pp. 2–3)

Deborah Bird Rose argues that for the Yarralin, Law is ultimately a cosmic principle which holds the world together, establishes relationships, orders reality, and sustains life.

> What Law seems most fundamentally to be about is relationships. Dreamings determined sets of moral relationships — country to country, country to plant and animal species, people to country, people to species, people to people. Individuals of any species come and go, but the underlying relationships persist. Law is a serious life and death business for individuals and for the world; it tells how the world hangs together. To disregard the Law would be to disregard the source of life and thus to allow the cosmos to fall apart. (Rose 1992, p. 56)

Law, then, is that comprehensive set of principles and rules imparted to the ancestors from the Spirit of the Land. Law is an eternal spiritual force upholding all physical, social and ceremonial realities. It is sad that immigrant Australians perceived so little of this indigenous system of relationships, and declared indigenous Australians to be such depraved and degraded specimens of humanity 'that they have reached the level of beasts, every thought bearing upon the nature of rational beings erased from their breasts' (Harris 1990, p. 31).

The challenge now is to recognise Aboriginal Law as a code of behaviour coexisting with 'white man's law'. Disputes over the hunting and fishing rights of Aboriginal communities, for example, revolve around a serious claim that traditional Law has not been extinguished and still has force. Pastor Davey Inkamala from Jay Creek in the Northern Territory sees no conflict between establishing this Law and the Gospel he preaches. For him reconciliation means two laws operating in concord. In an interview in 1997 he asserted:

we got Law for this country before white man came.
And that Law been handed over from history today to
us. We made the Law, our country Law, and we got to
take that Law to our government and show them —
look, sit down and we can make an agreement. These
two laws got to come together, and work together. And
we be like one nation then.

Many Aboriginal leaders, such as Djiniyini Gondarra, are
campaigning for an Act of Parliament which recognises
Aboriginal structures of Law and governance, and delegates
power to appropriate Aboriginal bodies in a given region.
While the process is complex, the principle of recognising
Aboriginal Law as a valid partner within the Australian legal
system represents a significant valuing that is consistent with
the justice principle enunciated in chapter 2.

Another aspect of valuing Aboriginal Law is recognising
that this Law is the work of the Spirit of the Land operating
in the indigenous context in much the same way as the
Creator was working in other cultures. The Spirit of the
Land was creating indigenous Law in this land long before
biblical laws were laid down. Charles Harris writes that the

fact that God was here in this land long before 1788
proves the fallacy of the missionaries who came out
and told the Aboriginal people that they were bringing
God to us. God was *already here* and with the people.
The Aboriginal Law is almost identical to the Mosaic
Law. God was here interacting with the Aboriginal and
Torres Strait Islander people and they interacted with
the Creator God, thereby receiving the law, values and
customs which have great biblical significance, for
instance the system of caring and sharing. (Harris
1996, p. 67)

The racist claims of the 18th and 19th centuries that 'the
principles of natural law' have been extinguished in indigenous

peoples must be rejected as totally false (Eze 1997, p. 93). Rather, I believe the time has come to value Aboriginal Law as a forceful spiritual and social reality in Aboriginal life. This eternal principle called Law 'holds together' all things and is far more than a quaint tribal belief. The Law is a profound principle that integrates society and creation, human life and all other life — both the spiritual and the material. Such a principle has something to offer all Australians in an age when human beings are in the process of polluting and destroying this planet. The Law, moreover, links everything with the land — this land — and leads us to search for the soul of this land in more than 'football, meat pies and Holden cars'.

The search

Australia's soul is linked to the Spirit of the Land. The Spirit of the Land points all Australians back to spiritual roots in this land, to that mysterious life force that emerged from this land and gave it form. The indigenous experience of the Spirit as the Spirit of the Land is to be valued, therefore, as more than a romantic ideal, or an object for academic analysis. The Spirit of the Land and indigenous Law have given a distinctive character to this country. I contend that when we as immigrant Australians also embrace these experiences as belonging to our roots and recognise how much we owe the Spirit of the Land, we become Australians who sense another deeper dimension of our soul than the explorer's romantic image of Australia Felix. Acknowledging our common spiritual roots in this way is not cultural appropriation, but cultural appreciation, and part of the search to discover who we are as Australians.

CHAPTER 6

KINSHIP WITH THE LAND

We who are Aboriginal Australian understand our
spiritual connectedness with the land. Christians have an
understanding of spirituality, and this is a place we can
journey together. I believe that Aboriginal people need to
acknowledge that other Australians born in this land have
tasted the spirituality of the land, even if they haven't
recognised it. (Djiniyini Gondarra, Council 1997a, p. 39)

*In this chapter I explore the significance of the land in the
reconciliation process, especially the spiritual dimension of
the land. In particular, my aim is to acknowledge not only
that indigenous Australians experience the land as the very
source of life and as the domain of the spiritual, but also that
immigrant Australians, born of this land, are invited to
empathise with the indigenous people who lost so much
when they lost the land. A mutual appreciation of the
spiritual in the land and the Spirit of the Land will help to
facilitate one of the aims of the Council for Aboriginal
Reconciliation: 'understanding country'.*

Farming the land

Have I, as an immigrant Australian, 'tasted the spirituality of the land' as Djiniyini Gondarra suggests in the quotation above? Can I discern the spiritual in the land? What kind of relationship did my farming forebears have with the land?

This land is my place, my country; I was born here. This is the land in which I am searching for the spiritual; I am not searching in some promised land of long ago or in some promised land in the hereafter. This land, where indigenous and non-indigenous Australians have a vision of reconciliation, is my land.

My great-grandparents were German immigrants seeking a piece of land they could call their own. Australia was the land of opportunity where the pain of the past could be forgotten. South Australia, in particular, was part of a popular dream to establish an ideal community grounded in 'Christian economics'. When they arrived my great-grandparents did not know that the local Kaurna of Adelaide or the Peramangk of the Barossa Valley had been excluded from this planned community. Nor did they discern, apparently, that this land of opportunity would soon become a land of oppression for these local inhabitants.

This ignorance on the part of our ancestors should not blind us to the fact that most of them were God-fearing people with a commitment to the land and their goal was to find land on which to make a new home. Having no money, my ancestors worked together at the goldfields for a short time to raise the capital to buy a small plot.

Between the shores of Lake Kennedy and Lake Linlithgow my great-grandparents 'put down their roots' and settled for life. They believed their piece of land was a gift from God. They were apparently unaware that it was stolen from the Aboriginal communities. They were told the Aborigines were 'rootless' nomads who spent their lives going 'walkabout'. They did not realise that the Aborigines were the custodians of the land and had a spiritual kinship with the land. When these pioneer men and women 'put down their roots', they entered an unwritten covenant in which their God unites land and farmer in a symbiotic relationship. These farming families believed that if they were faithful to the land, the land would be faithful in return. Many farmers have a type of 'land spirituality', a sense of God's presence when they 'worked the land' — though most of them would prefer not to talk about such things. A house, fences, sheds, an orchard, gardens and sometimes a grave or two were evidence that farming families had put down roots. They were committed to 'making a go of it' on the land — living on the land, dying on the land and returning to the earth of this land.

In their covenant with God, the farmers cleared, ploughed and sowed the land; God, in turn, was expected to bless it with rain, sunshine and fertility. They discerned the spiritual descending from heaven above — not from earth below — to animate the land. This agreement is reflected in an old hymn, written in 1861 by J.A.P. Schultz, and sung with gusto by my ancestors.

> We plough the fields and scatter
> The good seed on the land,
> But it is fed and watered
> By God's almighty hand;
> He sends the needed moisture,
> the warmth to swell the grain,
> The breezes and the sunshine
> And soft, refreshing rain.
>
> All good gifts around us
> Are sent from heaven above.
> Then thank the Lord, O thank the Lord
> For all his love. (*Lutheran Hymnal* 1973, p. 563)

After years of battling the harsh elements of the Australian seasons, farmers had a strong sense of belonging to the land, a kinship with the soil. Small farmers knew from bitter experience what it meant to be a 'battler', to be locked in a life-and-death struggle, in a war of survival with the forces of nature and society. Droughts and depressions, floods and financiers — each took their toll. But as true battlers do, they believed that if they kept faith with the land, the land would keep faith with them until they 'got on top of it'. They believed in the blessing that followed from farming the land in the way they believed 'God intended'. When I lived on the farm, I too had a sense that I belonged to the land where my family lived. That piece of land was — and still is — part of me.

> Within me I know
> a piece of land
> linking me,
> soul and soil,
> with other pieces
> of that living map
> I call my country.

Losing the land

It comes as a nasty shock when we immigrant Australians discover that the land we treasure and tend as home was once taken forcibly from another people whose names and stories are lost. It comes as an unwelcome surprise when we first realise that our God-fearing ancestors thanked God for their land as a precious gift when in fact it was stolen property.

The reality that we were 'invading' immigrants came very forcefully to me when I discovered that on Mengler's Hill in South Australia's Barossa Valley there is a line chiselled into a monument which reads, 'The Lord has given us this land' (Joshua 2:9). The German settlers quoted a text from the Hebrew Scriptures, justifying the conquest of Canaan by force, to thank God for the rich land they turned into vineyards. These settlers did not fully realise that their coming was a conquest; the local Aboriginal Australians clearly did. What it meant for Aboriginal Australians to lose their land — whether in the Barossa or Bankstown — may be something immigrant urban Australians today will never fully grasp. What it must have been like to be dispossessed by invaders who claimed to worship a loving God and 'love their neighbours as themselves' is hard to even imagine. I do not like to contemplate the desecration by axe and gun of a place held sacred, a place where dead are buried, a place where people's spiritual life rises from deep within the ground. Yet the pain of indigenous people's loss of land is an experience which we as immigrant Australians need to try to understand in the interests of justice and reconciliation.

Recent stories of battling farmers forced to leave their land when their banks foreclosed on their loans highlight that, for many rural people, their kinship with the land remains strong today. A collection of poems written by the local people on Kangaroo Island, South Australia, during a recent recession, illustrate their deep attachment to the land. A poem by Bev Wilson reveals a silent communion with place and paddock. Reading this poem reminds me of my own boyhood experience of walking through our property with my father, kicking at the earth with the toe of my boot, and feeling at one with the land.

> Yesterday we walked the hills —
> just Blue, the dog, and me.
> I said goodbye to the patient land,
> the hills, the trees and all my plans.
> We talked a bit as good friends do —
> the dog, the land, and me ...
> But now against the tree-lined hills,
> the new day's sky creeps pale and still,
> and I must face this coming day
> with knowledge of debts I cannot pay.
> (Gloyne 1992, p. 55)

The Aboriginal people's experience of losing their land is not simply a memory from a harsh and distant history. The pain and the anguish persist, as the poetry of many contemporary Aboriginal Australians testifies. The 'mother' they have lost still survives, but inhabited by someone else's children. Something of that pain is reflected in a poem by Jack Davis — he longs to be enfolded again by his mother, the land.

> Mother why don't you enfold me
> as you used to in the long long ago
> your morning breath
> was sweetness in my soul
> The daily scent of woodsmoke
> was a benediction in the air
> The coolness when you
> wore your cloak of green
> after the rain was mine
> all mine to cherish and survey
> Then the other came
> and ripped the soil
> and plagued our hearts
> yours and mine
> The benediction became a curse
> of cloven hooves
> whip chain and gun
> The sun became to me a blood red orb
> Nails and flesh fell away
> leaving only
> whitening bones bare in the summer sun
> My voice cries thinly in the dark night
> mother oh mother
> why don't you enfold me
> as you used to, in the long long ago.
> (Davis 1992, p. 6)

RECONCILIATION

One of the most painful aspects of the poems written by Aboriginal people is that the religion of those immigrants who intended to bring a blessing to the land is experienced as integral to the loss and desecration of the land. The 'loving God' of these immigrants had no love for those inhabitants who did not farm 'as God intended'. The spirituality of the invaders was, for many Aborigines, experienced as alien to the Spirit of the Land and the people of the land. Mary Duroux writes of the land as being 'crucified'.

> My mother, my Mother
> what have they done?
> Crucified you
> like the Only Son.
> Murder committed
> by mortal hand.
> I weep, my mother,
> my mother, the land.
> (Duroux 1992, p. 20)

Aboriginal writers often portray losing the land as losing a mother: their source of life, identity and place in the world. Losing the land is experienced as death. Seeing the land violated is viewed as rape. Being removed from the land is understood as exile. Ironically, in his poem Jack Davis calls the immigrant invaders 'the other', the alienating destroyers. Given the language used to describe these experiences, it may be difficult for us immigrant Australians to empathise with indigenous Australians — especially since many of our ancestors immigrated here so long ago. Yet, if the reconciliation process is to be more than superficial, I believe that those of us who have a sense of kinship with this land also need to empathise with indigenous Australians and acknowledge the trauma of losing the land, especially land experienced as 'my mother'.

The land as spiritual

There are numerous books and articles by non-indigenous anthropologists and indigenous Australians about the spiritual nature of the land in Aboriginal culture. My concern here is not to cover again the range of ideas relating to those spiritual links that have been identified in different Aboriginal communities across Australia. My goal is to highlight that the land is experienced by Aboriginal peoples as spiritual and to explore the significance of that spiritual experience for immigrant Australians — both in terms of our relationship with this land and our concern for justice for the surviving indigenous peoples of this land.

The primacy of land in the life and spirituality of Aboriginal people is expressed forcefully by Michael Dodson when he speaks of the need to 'begin with the land'.

> To understand our law, our culture and our
> relationship to the physical and spiritual world, you
> must begin with the land. Everything about Aboriginal
> society is inextricably interwoven with, and connected
> to, the land. Culture is the land, the land and
> spirituality of Aboriginal people, our cultural beliefs or
> reason for existence is the land. You take that away
> and you take away our reason for existence. We have
> grown the land up. We are dancing, singing and
> painting for the land. We are celebrating the land.
> Removed from our lands, we are literally removed from
> ourselves. (M. Dodson, 1997, p. 41)

In Arnhem Land, according to Galarrwuy Yunupingu, the spirit of a baby is believed to be born in a particular water hole; the spirit then enters the mother. 'The land gives a spirit to that baby and that baby will be a baby of that country.' The land is the spiritual mother; the land is the source of spiritual life and the spirit binds each person for life to the 'country' from which the spirit emerged (Yunupingu 1996, pp. 5–7).

The Aranda of central Australia believe that the spirit, or
'second soul', as Strehlow defines it, enters the pregnant
mother with her first bout of morning sickness, or with the
first stabs of pain within her womb, or when she has a dream
of the future child brought on by a ancestor being seeking
rebirth. According to Strehlow, '[e]ach person's second "soul"
therefore was a part of the total living immortal essence of a
totemic ancestor or ancestress who had sought reincarnation
in a new human being' (Strehlow 1971, p. 616).

The way the spirit of an individual relates to the spiritual
world within the land may vary from one community to
another. Aboriginal spirituality necessarily means that the
spirit of a person is linked to the spiritual world within the
land, a particular place in the land, and a particular ancestor.

> We all come from the land and that is where we will go
> back when we die. My bones will join those of my
> ancestors, so I feel I am part of a link that started over
> 60,000 years ago and will go on forever. (Yunupingu
> 1996, p. 6)

Many Aboriginal communities' stories recall how, in the
beginning, the ancestor beings or creator beings also emerged
from the land — or in some cases the sea. These emerging
spiritual forces walked the land, transformed the landscape,
and returned to the land where their spiritual presence
persists for all time. The entire landscape is filled with the
trails and sites where these creator beings travelled. The
country becomes a story written on the land for those who
know how to read the land. Myers summarises this spiritual
dimension of the landscape among the Pintubi people.

> The actions of these powerful beings — animal, human
> and monster — created the world as it now exists.
> They gave it outward form, identity (a name), and
> internal structure. The desert is crisscrossed with lines
> of travel and, just as animal tracks leave a record of

what happened, the geography and special features of
the land — hills, creeks, salt lakes, trees — are marks
of the ancestors' activities. Places where exceptionally
significant events took place, where power was left
behind, or where the ancestors went into the ground
and still remain, are special sacred sites (*yarta yarta*)
because ancestral potency is near. (Myers 1986, p. 50)

Sacred sites where 'ancestral potency is near' are those
places in the landscape where direct access to the spiritual
world of the land is gained and sustained through ritual and
story. Violation of these sites means severing that access to
the spiritual and violating the sacredness of the place. The
full force of this loss can hardly be imagined. Cecil Grant
states that 'one of the saddest things it [dispossession]
brought was disconnection with our spiritual heritage'. That
heritage, he says,

was handed down faithfully in a connected, unbroken
line, through initiation from generation to generation
for thousands of years until around the turn of the
century when it was broken. The impact of invasion,
the corruptions of colonisation, broke that connection.
(Pattel-Gray & Brown 1997, p. 3)

The struggle of Aboriginal people today, partly through
the process of reconciliation, is to restore, where possible,
these broken relationships with the land and the Spirit of the
Land. This involves communities making connection with
the spiritual world of their country. The struggle for land
rights is part of the struggle to restore these spiritual
connections.

The land as suffering

The land experienced by Aboriginal people as a spiritual
mother 'feeds and nurtures all the time, just like mothers

always look after their children ... That is why Aboriginal people sing about land, dance about land, tell stories about land — because we have such a belonging to the land' (Yunupingu 1996, p. 7). Just like a human mother, the land responds to the rites and experiences of those whom the land embraces.

The suffering of the land, says Yunupingu, is communicated to those who are sensitive to the language of the land.

> Even when I am not on my tribal land I am able to speak sign language; just like people who don't speak each other's languages have always communicated in sign language. I do the same thing by looking at the hills with no trees. I understand that maybe those hills are suffering a bit. I understand that Mother earth is suffering because there is so much devastation. Trees are dying and have to be cleared away, lands are being cut by floodwaters, and many other types of environmental destruction are taking place. That is when you experience the suffering of the Spirit of the Land because of the carelessness of the non-Aboriginal people who call themselves 'owners' of this country. (Yunupingu 1996, pp. 9–10)

The suffering of the land because of pollution and desecration is a theme in the biblical prophets that has not been taken seriously by most Christian immigrants to this land. Yet, as the prophet Jeremiah suggests, when the land suffers, God suffers (Habel 1996, p. 5). Or, in the words of Yunupingu, 'the Spirit of the Land' suffers because of the folly of non-Aboriginal 'owners'. The suffering of the land reflects the suffering of that spiritual presence in the land that some have called the Creator Spirit. However specific writers may designate this Spirit of the Land, Yunupingu confronts us with the reality that we non-indigenous peoples have caused the Spirit of the Land to suffer.

Can we, as non-indigenous peoples, hear the crying of the land as the crying of the Spirit of the Land? Are our spirits also capable of being in tune with the spiritual in this land? Can we empathise with the Rainbow Spirit Elders' understanding of the suffering Spirit.

> The Creator Spirit is crying because the deep spiritual bonds with the land and its people have been broken. The land is crying because it is slowly dying without this bond of spiritual life. The people are crying because they long for a restoration of that deep spiritual bond with the Creator Spirit and the land. (Rainbow Spirit Elders 1997, p. 42)

Those of us who are immigrant Australians may not have experienced direct spiritual connections with specific places in the same way as indigenous people. We may not believe we have links with the spiritual stories and sites of a particular part of the country in the same way. I suspect, however, that if we accept the challenge of Djiniyini Gondarra, many of us will admit to an awareness of what Yunupingu calls the Spirit of the Land, and perhaps even the suffering of that Spirit. Gondarra's challenge, implicit in the lead quote of this chapter, is clear.

> I want to challenge my Aboriginal brothers and sisters to recognise our unique spirituality and fight for its survival. I'm saying to other Australians, 'If you are born of this land, you've tasted its spirituality, but what have you done with that?' Indigenous people have cared for this land for maybe 100,000 years; in the last 200 its spirituality has been ignored as it has been progressively raped.
> Reconciliation, friends, is about healing the scars on the land and within the land, and within us as Australians — indigenous and others. (Council 1997b, Book 2, p. 72)

117

Gondarra invites non-indigenous Australians to recognise that though people such as myself have an immigrant heritage, we are also 'born of this land'. We are not branded as invaders — even though that may have been true of some of our ancestors. We are addressed as people of the land who can potentially understand something of the culture and experience of indigenous peoples also 'born of this land'.

Gondarra's challenge is also an invitation to recognise the spiritual in this land, something we may have already tasted unawares. Again, we are not set apart as Western Christians whose knowledge of the spiritual has been associated with a 'Father who art in heaven', inviting pilgrims to leave the 'earthly' land for a better place in heaven. Discerning the spiritual in the land as the Spirit of the Land is presented as a mutual possibility and a pathway to 'understanding country'. Following that path will help facilitate reconciliation. Discerning the Spirit of the Land leads to discerning the suffering of the Spirit. The suffering of the Spirit of the Land commenced with the invasion, persisted through 200 years of racist sin, and continues today with the environmental degradation of the land. For those of us less in tune with the language of the earth, the cries of the indigenous people may mediate the cries of the land (Habel 1996, p. 10). For others, the suffering of the Spirit of the Land can be linked with the suffering of God at Calvary, and seen as a spiritual continuation of that suffering presence in the Australian landscape.

Native title

It is not appropriate for me to enter the discussion about the precise legal meaning of the concept of 'native title' in common law as people such as Noel Pearson have done (1997). More significant in this context is that some indigenous people use the term 'native title' as a symbol for justice in the reconciliation process — as the collection of papers commemorating twenty years of progress since the *Aboriginal Land Rights Act 1976* clearly illustrates. William Deane, Governor-General of Australia at that time, says in the preface '[this book] shows us there is a way forward towards reconciliation on the basis of friendship and equality between the Australian nation and its indigenous peoples' (Yunupingu 1997, p. x). Galarrwuy Yunupingu highlights how the notion of native title has become a symbol of Aboriginal Law and culture and much more than a legal concept.

> Native Title is not a piece of paper or words in a book. It is our living Aboriginal culture. It is our songs and our dances, painted on our bodies and written in the sand. It is our law which has been unchanged for thousands of years.
> If it is taken away then everything is lost. And Australia has lost its last chance for reconciliation. Our children should be able to grow up equal, as mates, in a fair country. Killing off our law and culture will make this impossible. (Council 1997a, Book 1, p. 39)

The *Native Title Act 1993* validated the 1992 decision of the High Court of Australia (*Queensland v Mabo No. 2*), which held that, among other things,

> the doctrine of *terra nullius* has no application to lands which were inhabited or occupied by Australian indigenous people — consequently, the traditional rights of indigenous people to land survived the acquisition of sovereignty by the Crown; the common law recognises these traditional rights as a form of native title, subject to any extinguishment arising from legislation or executive action; the nature and content of a native title is ascertained by reference to the traditional laws and customs of indigenous people. (Yunupingu 1997, p. 235)

The significance of this decision is that, for the first time in 200 years, indigenous people can come to the negotiating table 'with legally recognised rights to land and resources' (Ridgeway 1997, p. 65). What Aboriginal people had always believed to be true under their own Law was now acknowledged in Australian law. Now they had the 'right to negotiate' in cases relating to their land — their social and spiritual home. Any attempt to tamper with the Act, or the subsequent Wik decision based on this Act, was viewed by indigenous Australians as negating Aboriginal rights and sabotaging the reconciliation process. Upholding native title, therefore, represents justice; as such it is a necessary prerequisite for reconciliation. Land rights ought not be reduced to a legal and political game. This process relates to the land, the very source of the spiritual reality known to Aboriginal people.

The search

I accept the implied challenge of Djiniyini Gondarra to acknowledge the spirituality 'other Australians born in this land have tasted'. That spirituality, I believe, belongs to Australia's soul. I may not have experienced the Spirit in the same way that indigenous peoples have known the Spirit of the Land. I may not have been as acutely aware of the suffering of the Spirit and the land as indigenous Australians. Whether my heritage is linked with pioneer farmers, urban settlers or indigenous ancestors, I am linked with this land as a spiritual place.

CHAPTER 7

SHAME, SORRY AND
FORGIVENESS

And every morning when the sun came up the whole
family would wail. They did that for 32 years until they
saw me again. Who can imagine what a mother went
through? But you have to learn to forgive. (Plaque at the
Fountain of Tears, Adelaide)

*The forgiveness factor introduced in chapter 2 is here applied
to the reconciliation process. A distinction is made between
guilt and shame as possible responses to past injustices
against indigenous Australians. I discuss apologies as
necessary to the forgiveness process and offer a possible
model for an apology focusing on the seven sins against
indigenous Australians outlined earlier. I analyse the process
of forgiveness as a power for healing in the Australian
context.*

Shame and guilt

I remember one Sunday — I was still a teenager — when the respected parents of a teenage girl asked to speak to the local congregation after the worship service had finished. What followed was very painful. They 'confessed' to the whole congregation publicly that their daughter had 'fallen pregnant out of wedlock' and would have a child in several months. In their eyes — and the eyes of most of the congregation — their daughter had sinned. Instead of hiding the sin by sending their daughter out of town as I knew others had done, these parents made a 'full confession' before their friends.

They concluded their painful story by asking forgiveness from the congregation and requesting their acceptance back into the community. The parents, not the daughter, were asking for forgiveness and healing. 'We feel guilty about what our daughter has done and we ask you to forgive us and accept us.' Only upon reflection did I realise that what these parents felt was shame not guilt, yet they expressed their 'confession' in terms of guilt. Their daughter had 'sinned' in the eyes of the community and the parents felt ashamed. Their shame was so great that they could not keep silent and hide it. If they had kept silent, they said, their guilt would have continued to consume them.

Shame and guilt are two quite different human responses. Guilt over a given sin may be forgiven in a formal act, but the shame may continue for generations and the wounds take much longer to heal. Guilt and shame may both be responses to a particular event. Though I may not feel guilty, I may feel shame for the actions associated with me in some way. I may feel shame for many things, including what others have done — whether family, friends, community, church or nation. I may not be individually guilty of perpetrating an action, but may still feel ashamed of what happened. If I have a right to be proud of my community or nation, am I not morally obliged to feel ashamed of the brutal injustices in Australia's past? Or, as Gaita writes, the 'wish for national pride without the possibility of national shame is an expression of that corrupt attachment to a collective whose name is jingoism' (1998, p. 14).

Pride is the opposite of shame. As members of an Australian community, many of us happily identify with past events or periods in which we take pride. At the Olympic Games most Australians take pride in the exploits of Australian athletes. On Anzac Day many Australians take pride in the courage of those who fought for their country. In many contexts Australians share a communal pride. They do not say, I was not there; I did not personally perform heroic deeds. But if I as an Australian am privileged to celebrate Australia's communal pride, surely I am morally obligated to express Australia's communal shame.

Understanding the distinction between guilt and shame is crucial in the current reconciliation struggle. The recent report on the stolen generation evoked two very opposite responses locally. Some felt deep shame and participated in various ceremonies where they made a formal apology and said 'sorry'. Others, such as local high school students I encountered, asserted quite vigorously 'I didn't do it. I'm not personally guilty.' 'I didn't commit any of these sins against Aborigines. I don't need to say sorry.'

Legally speaking, almost all of us living today were not the actual perpetrators of the many crimes against Aboriginal peoples over the past 200 years. We did not invade and steal Aboriginal land. We did not poison their flour and waterholes. We did not commit genocide. We did not steal children from their parents to make them 'white'. We did not do it. So we cannot be taken to court and charged. We are innocent!

Unlike the situation for the victims presenting their case before the Truth and Reconciliation Commission in South Africa, some of the crimes against Aboriginal peoples reach back more than 200 years — to 1788. Does that mean they should be ignored? Does that mean Australians should 'let bygones be bygones' and only plan for the future? Does that mean Australians should bury their past history and not face their collective conscience? Far from it!

The need to speak of individual or even communal guilt about what happened in the past is disputed in the current debate. As Pat Dodson and others at the 1997 Australian Reconciliation Convention publicly declared,

> individual Australians are not guilty for what happened
> to our families. But if you fail to respond to what you
> know that will be another thing. If you do not help to
> ease the pain, that will be your act for which you are
> responsible. (Council 1997c, Book 3, p. 33)

How should we respond? In an earlier chapter I spoke of the need to face the story of what happened in the past and acknowledge the seven sins committed against indigenous people at suffering sites around the country. How do we as immigrant Australians, whose roots reach back fifty years or more, respond to these stories, to these bloody realities from our common history?

With shame! The first response I believe immigrant Australians ought to make is a genuine expression of shame for the brutal crimes committed against indigenous Australians at all the suffering sites around the country. For me to avoid the shame of Australia's past would, I propose, be to deny my very identity as an Australian, and involve me in an attempt to crush my own conscience. To do so would be to separate myself from all the rest of the people of this land because of these atrocities in Australia's history. I am part of a community, a people of which I am proud. But I am also part of a community, a people with a bloody past. This past contributes to my sense of communal shame, whether I try to hide it or not.

Part of the moral imperative of being Australian, I believe, is to acknowledge Australia's shame: the tragic suffering inflicted on the indigenous few. Those of us still associated with the church know, it seems to me, a double shame. The church and missions who should have provided strong moral leadership were often complicit in many unjust government policies, such as the removal and institutionalising of Aboriginal children. Some missionaries may have saved Aboriginal groups from the police — and I am glad they did. Some may have prevented whole communities from being exterminated — and I am glad they did. But when the police brought stolen children to some missionaries, they were also accepted and in most cases treated as servants — some missionaries were actively complicit in depriving these children of their identity, name and culture.

It is time to say more than sorry. It is time to say, 'as an Australian I am ashamed of what happened'.

Apologies and confessions

How, in the interests of reconciliation, should I as an immigrant Australian express my sense of shame and anguish about the sins of past generations? What kind of formal apology, confession or occasion is required? What ultimately is the purpose of an apology? As a number of writers have noted, in public affairs apologies are relatively recent acts of repentance. In countries such as South Africa, the spiritual process of repentance, confession and reconciliation found in the Christian tradition has been extended into the national spotlight. A traditionally Christian process has been moved from the private confessional into the public domain. The power of the process, however, can still transform even in the public and communal sphere.

What then are the essential features of such an apology? First, the offending party publicly articulates the hidden or suppressed history, including the wrongs that have been committed. Second, those making the apology express their shame and begin the process of identifying publicly with the suffering victims. To apologise is to empathise. Third, an apology is a public declaration that those apologising are seeking reconciliation. Apologies are designed to break down alienation. According to Wink,

> Tavuchis concludes that the principal function of an apology is precisely its putting in the public record a statement of awareness and intent that seeks reconciliation, whether it has the power to accomplish that or not, and whether it is accepted or not. (Wink 1998, p. 56)

Contrary to the perception of some cynics, an apology is not simply a matter of 'saying sorry and getting it over with'. An apology involves struggling with the brutal sins of the past, finding words that express genuine sorrow, and facing the very people who have been brutalised. With the words, moreover, comes a commitment to changed behaviour that is 'more than words'. With a genuine apology comes a concern for justice and the chance for a better way to live together in the future.

As a consequence of the release of the *Inquiry into the Separation of Aboriginal and Torres Strait Islander Children from their Families* in 1997, a significant number of groups in Australian society have made public apologies. The Australian Catholic Social Justice Council apology included expressions such as 'we feel great sorrow,' 'we are truly sorry,' and 'we regret'. The members of the council expressed the hope that by telling the 'truth' about the past they would be taking a step toward healing. The Australian Catholic Bishops Conference also issued a formal apology and specifically asked 'the victims of the policy of breaking up indigenous families for their forgiveness for any part the Church may have played in causing their harm and suffering' (Manning 1998, no 89, p. 4).

The South Australian synod of the Uniting Church in Australia went a step further in their apology at the October

1997 assembly in Adelaide. The assembly formally 'confessed' the collaboration of the church with the government in its child-seizure policies, 'apologised' for the pain inflicted on so many families and 'pledged' itself to solidarity with, and justice for, Aboriginal Australians. Somewhat belated, but no less significant, is the apology of the South Australian legal fraternity in September 1998; their statement not only 'acknowledges with deepest regret the various government policies that sought to assimilate Aboriginal people into Australian society' but also formally recognises that 'for tens of thousands of years before this country was colonised, Aboriginal people enjoyed their own forms of government and law' (*The Advertiser*, 10 September 1998, p. 6).

Whatever the precise wording of a given apology, the report on the 'stolen children' provided the impetus for a series of apologies relating to concrete policies that have affected Aboriginal people who are still alive. These apologies are important steps in the ongoing reconciliation process.

Two questions still concern me. Why do these apologies avoid confessing communal shame for past injustices? And should similar apologies focusing on the other evils perpetrated against the indigenous peoples of Australia be forthcoming? Or should such deep memories be left buried?

As others have done, I, as a fellow human being, would like to say that I am not only sorry about the many atrocities that happened in Australia's past, but that I am also ashamed of what the authorities, communities and leaders of my country did to other human beings — to Aboriginal Australians. I am ashamed of how my people stole Aboriginal lands and, by removing Aboriginal people from their lands, disconnected their sacred ties with their land. I am ashamed of how we attempted genocide in the Black War of Tasmania. I am ashamed of how we murdered Aborigines by poisoning food rations and waterholes. I am ashamed of the racist beliefs that tolerated and allowed such evils, beliefs that I inherited and held for many years. Yes, I am ashamed.

I believe, too, that as immigrant Australians we need to apologise for more than the assimilation policy that led to the forceful removal of Aboriginal children. We need to confess each of the injustices represented by the seven suffering sites I have identified above, and make apologies modelled, perhaps, on the one given at the end of this chapter. How and when this should be done may be a matter for discussion in each community. Apologies ought to be made after due and honest reflection, at appropriate occasions, as part of symbolic events, and on days of social or national significance.

Effective apologies demand a sense of public occasion. It is not insignificant that when the last tsar was laid to rest in St Petersburg in July 1998, the occasion was the eightieth anniversary of his execution and the beginning of the communist era. At that ceremony President Boris Yeltsin formally acknowledged the sin and shame of Russia's past.

We must tell the truth — the [tsar's] massacre has become one of the most shameful pages of our history ... By burying the remains of the innocent victims we want to expiate the sins of our ancestors. [This burial is] an act of human justice, a symbol of unity of the people, of collective guilt.' (*The Advertiser*, 18 July 1998, p. 45)

Whether or not the burial of the tsar's remains constituted expiation may be debated. Public confession of the shame, however, was abundantly clear. The deep memory and the collective shame of the Russians was publicly acknowledged in a symbolic act that reached deep into the psyche of the nation. I believe Australians need to do some deep remembering about our common history to enable the spectres of our past misdeeds to be laid to rest — named and confessed but not forgotten.

In some countries, deep remembering has erupted in revenge because the original wounds were never healed.

Geiko Mueller-Fahrenholz argues that when the Serbian leader Slobodan Milosevic headed the celebrations to commemorate the 600th anniversary of the Battle of Kosovo in 1989, he created within the Serbian people a new remembering of their identity as heroic victims defending their Christian values against Turkish infidels. This process of selective remembering has been linked to the ethnic cleansing which followed the outbreak of war in the former Yugoslavia soon after these celebrations. 'Six hundred years had not sufficed to heal the traumatic wounds caused by that defeat on the Kosovo' (Mueller-Fahrenholz 1997, p. 46).

The wounds inflicted on the Aboriginal peoples still need to be healed; 200 years of injustices are enough! Before we devolve into 'battles' in the law courts or the parliament, I am convinced that Australians with a conscience need to confess Australia's shame and seek healing, a healing that may include forgiveness.

Forgiveness

I deliberately used the word 'may' in this connection, because those of us who dare to make an apology ought not assume that the victims are obligated to forgive. The anguish of researching, formulating and publicly confessing shame or sorrow over a deep memory is no guarantee that the offended party will forgive or accept the apology. Walter Wink reports how in 1986, the United Church of Canada made an apology to the native people of Canada for past wrongs inflicted upon them by the church, and asked forgiveness. There was apparently great happiness in the native council tepee when the apology was issued. Two years later, however, the governing council for native peoples within the church officially responded to the apology by 'acknowledging it but not accepting it'. Rather than being a damper, this action served as a basis for greater dignity and autonomy for Native Americans in the United Church of Canada (Wink 1998, p. 55).

Michael Henderson, who wrote a book entitled *The Forgiveness Factor*, legitimately asks whether forgiveness, an action which many of us associate with Christian worship and intimate personal relationships, is really out of place in the social and political context.

> Is forgiveness — both asking and offering — a realistic philosophy between nations and between individuals? Given the track record of this century, the cruelty, the senseless killing, the holocaust and genocide, one's scepticism about its possibility and efficacy is justified. The stories in this book, however, show that forgiveness, like hatred, knows no national boundaries and has the power to break vicious cycles of hatred and revenge. (Henderson 1996, pp. xix–xx)

Where a formal public apology is accepted and/or forgiveness is spoken by one or more representatives of the aggrieved party, the healing process begins and new partnerships can be formed; the same applies in the political arena. The act of forgiveness may be both cathartic for the sufferer as well as a release for the perpetrator, as the Truth and Reconciliation Commission in South Africa testifies.

> There is deep satisfaction of course. Those destined to be annihilated are now praised as heroes. When they were tortured in the prisons they were told: 'Yell as loud as you wish; nobody will ever hear you!' Well, now the whole nation hears, and the accounts of its sufferings are received into its memories ... This profound satisfaction is not a subliminal form of revenge, but expresses itself in genuine readiness to forgive. Many victims repeat the phrase expressed by a witness during the first days of the hearings: 'I am ready to forgive, but I need to know whom and for what'. (Mueller-Fahrenholz 1997, p. 89)

The situation in Australia is different, but no less susceptible to the impact of forgiveness. Subsequent to the apologies made for the part played by governments, communities and churches in the forcible removal of children from their Aboriginal families, a number of public statements of forgiveness have been offered by Aboriginal leaders who were themselves 'stolen' children. Those words of forgiveness continue to facilitate reconciliation.

The words quoted at the head of this chapter are the sentiments recorded on a plaque beside the Fountain of Tears sculpture in Adelaide on the site of the Colebrook Home 'orphanage' for stolen children. They are the words of an Aboriginal mother who has waited for thirty-two years to find her family and finally heal the memory by forgiving her abductors.

I was present at several apologies in 1998, including the one expressed by the Blackwood community at the Fountain of Tears. Lowitja O'Donoghue, herself one of the stolen children, accepted a public apology by the local community and extended forgiveness on behalf the Aboriginal people involved. The words were powerful. The generosity of spirit, the absence of revenge, and a vision for healing relationships were features I felt deeply — as did others present on those occasions. The word 'we forgive', however, had the greatest impact. For me, those words transformed a community occasion into a spiritual occasion. The spirit of the Aboriginal people who had suffered under the inhuman policy of assimilation reached out to my spirit when they forgave me and my community for any part in that sin. For me, that experience was healing and moving.

I want to go a step further and say that this spiritual occasion was for me an experience of the Spirit of the Land at work in the community, healing and bonding two alienated groups of Australians. Or in terms of the Christian Scriptures, this is an extension of the work of the suffering God. The power behind these communal acts of forgiveness that break down barriers erected by Australia's sins is the cross — the healing power released by the suffering of God.

The search

In these continuing acts of forgiveness I see a spirit of grace and goodwill, of compassion and fair play, of generosity and earthy humanity, rising from within this land and reflecting a profound aspect of the Australian soul that Aboriginal people are sharing with us. Australia is more than a country with two cultures in conflict, more than a common history of atrocities. Australia is a country whose soul is also being formed by the forgiving spirit of its indigenous peoples. Perhaps the epitome of this hope is reflected in a speech given at a thanksgiving rally on Elcho Island in 1979; the Aboriginal leader spoke with passion. 'One day in the not too distant future an Aboriginal Australian will be prime minister of this land. And the first words he will speak to the nation are simply, "We forgive you".'

An apology

The apology which follows is based on the seven sins identified in an earlier chapter as integral to our shared history and our corporate search for who we are as Australians. Some readers may find them appropriate and use them individually or together, perhaps in connection with the healing rites at seven sites outlined in the Appendix. Others may wish to include details more specific to the crimes of a given locality.

Indigenous brothers and sisters,
for the sin of dispossession I am ashamed, because
from early in our common history, government authorities and immigrant settlers stole from you your land, your home, your mother. They cleared, ploughed and fenced your land and made you homeless. They 'farmed' your land, they claimed, 'as God intended'. They dispossessed you. They did not really care that it was your land, your mother.

For the sin of genocide I am ashamed because
from early in our common history, certain
government authorities and police bodies pursued
a policy of genocide — either waiting for your
people to die out or actively helping you disappear
through murder and dispossession. In the Black
War in Tasmania, soldiers, police and settlers
combined in one black line to erase your people
from your land — because you were in the way of
'progress'. They did not care that you were
custodians of the land.

For the sin of massacre I am ashamed because
from early in our common history, police and
community bodies, following a policy of
'dispersal', conducted raids on Aboriginal camps
in retaliation for minor offences. They massacred
unarmed men, women and children without
mercy, sometimes burning or burying them to hide
the evidence. They did it, they said, 'to teach you a
lesson'. They did not care about your fragile lives.

For the sin of dehumanisation I am ashamed because
from early in our common history, Australian
authorities followed a policy of treating you like
livestock, giving you rations at 'feeding stations'
on the fringes of farms and communities. They
also tolerated settlers or police poisoning your
waterholes and lacing your flour with arsenic
when you 'became a problem'. They did not care
about your hurting humanity.

*For the sin of destroying your culture I am ashamed
because*
from early in our common history, government
authorities, in cooperation with local and
mission bodies, removed Aboriginal groups
surviving in their own lands, exiled them in
reserves or missions, and forced them to abandon

their culture, their language, their so-called 'savage' ways and so become 'civilised'. They tried to crush your Aboriginal spirit. They did not care about your Aboriginal soul — even if some missions sought to save your 'immortal soul'.

For the sin of desecration I am ashamed because from early in our common history government authorities and immigrant settlers have desecrated your sacred lands, your sacred sites, your sacred ancestors. In the 1950s the Australian government even helped the British government desecrate lands with atomic fallout to 'keep the country free'. Meanwhile sacred shrines called churches were built on your sacred land without permission. They did not care about your sacred sites.

For the sin of assimilation I am ashamed because through much of our common history in the 20th century, government authorities fostered a policy of assimilation, seeking to fade indigenous black faces into the landscape of white society. In line with this policy, police forcibly removed Aboriginal children, especially so-called 'half-caste' children, from their parents' arms and placed them in so-called orphanages to civilise them and make them white. They did not care about your true identity.

I am very ashamed of these sins from the past,
and I am profoundly sorry for the injustices
committed against Aboriginal Australians.
Indigenous Australians, please accept my apology.
Spirit of the Land, forgive me
and my Australian brothers and sisters.

CHAPTER 8

SYMBOLS OF SUFFERING AND HEALING

To put it in scriptural terms, Aboriginal people may
represent for us the Suffering Servant 'wounded for our
iniquities and bruised for our sins'. (Brady 1998, p. 91)

*As an advocate of reconciliation I have, in this book,
identified seven representative sites where indigenous
Australians have suffered at the hands of immigrant
Australians since 1788. I have specified seven sins committed
against Aboriginal Australians at these sites and have
confessed my shame at these destructive events in Australian
history. I have acknowledged the Aboriginal experience of
the Spirit of the Land as integral to our Australian identity
— both social and spiritual. I now ask how the Spirit of the
Land was involved in the suffering of the Aboriginal people
during the atrocities and injustices outlined above. I will
focus on the painful story of the stolen children who have
become, in my opinion, a significant symbol of suffering and
healing for both Aboriginal and non-Aboriginal people.*

The stolen children

Colebrook Home once stood just up the road from where I now live in Adelaide. For years, I, like most other residents, had no idea of what the house represented. We had no idea that this house was a symbol of an Australian policy that created the stolen generation. We had no idea that the Colebrook Home 'orphans', who went to Blackwood School, were not orphans at all, but Aboriginal children stolen from their families and relocated in this institution in order to turn them into 'good Aussies'. We had no idea that this house was a house of sadness and suffering. And we could hardly imagine how significant the story of these stolen children would become for many Australians.

There are numerous suffering sites like Colebrook Home scattered throughout Australia. The story of these sites and the people who suffered in them is recorded in the inquiry chaired by Sir Ronald Wilson: *Bringing Them Home. The Report of the National Inquiry into the Separation of Aboriginal and Torres Strait Islander Children from Their Families*. The stories of children taken forcibly from their parents included in this report are heart-wrenching and cruel. The suffering of both parents and children is illustrated in the following example.

> I do remember my mother showing up for visits, supervised visits. We used to get excited. I just wanted her to take us away from there. Then the visits just stopped. I'm told the authorities stopped them because she had a destabilising effect on us.
>
> That didn't deter my mother. She used to come to the school ground to visit us over the fence. The authorities found out about those visits. They had to send us to a place where she couldn't get to us. To send us anywhere on mainland Queensland, she would have just followed — so they sent us to the one place where

she can't follow: Palm Island Aboriginal Settlement.
By our mother visiting us illegally at that school ground
she unknowingly sealed our fate. I wasn't to see my
mother again for ten nightmare years. (Bird 1998,
p.43–4)

The suffering of the stolen children continued in the homes and institutions where they were 'imprisoned'. With that 'imprisonment' they lost their freedom, their rights, their culture and their identity. They lost, above all, the experience of having parents, of knowing the bonds of love between a child and a mother or a father. They lost their parents — and sometimes even the memory of them. I recall an elderly man in Hopevale who told us how, as a little boy, he would lie in the dark with the other children and try to imagine the face of his mother. He would try to imagine her face in the night. But slowly the image faded until he could remember her no longer. The image was gone. She was gone.

Some of the stories of these children are recorded in more detail in *The Stolen Children, Their Stories*. Whatever the pain of institutional life, the act of being wrenched from a mother remains perhaps the most horrendous crime of all. As Carmel Bird writes, the

stolen children in this book speak of a feeling of
emptiness, of having a hole in their hearts as they recall
the loss of family, language, culture and identity. They
catalogue the abuses at the hands of white families and
missionaries, but the original wound is that which was
inflicted at the moment they were torn from their
mothers. (Bird 1998, p. 10)

I do not have the space here to outline the numerous sins committed against these Aboriginal children. These wrongs range from virtual enslavement as servants in white households to imprisonment in rigid religious institutions. Rarely did these children know genuine affection or encouragement. They were frequently reduced to little more than regimented animals, often living in the most appalling conditions. Those in the homes were often totally isolated from the outside world and subjected to frequent floggings. They were wrenched from their lands, their communities, their spiritual homes. John's story illustrates something of the racism and dehumanisation involved.

I was definitely not told that I was Aboriginal. What the Sisters told us was that we had to be white. It was drummed into us that we were white. It did not matter what shade you were. We thought we were white. They said you can't talk to any of them coloured people because you're white ...

None of the other kids had visits from their parents. No visits from family. The worst part is, we didn't know we had family.

When you got to a certain age, like I got to ten years old ... they just told us we were going on a train trip ... We all lined up with our little ports [school cases] with a bible inside. That's all that was in the ports, see. We really treasured that, we thought it was a good thing that we had something ... The old man from La Perouse took us from Sydney, well actually from Bomaderry, to Kinchela Boys' Home. That's when our problems really started, you know!

This is where we learned we weren't white. First of all they took you in through the iron gates and took our little ports off us. Stick it in the fire with your little bible inside. They took us around to a room and shaved our hair off ... They gave you clothes and stamped a number on them ... They never called you by your name; they called you by your number. That number was stamped on everything.

Kinchela was [a] place where they thought you were animals. You know it was like a place where they go

round and kick us like a dog ... It was just like a prison.
Truthfully there were boys having sex with boys ... but
these other dirty mongrels didn't care. (Bird 1998, p. 63)

Physical and sexual abuse was common practice and left
many children broken in body as well as spirit. The crime of
attempting to destroy the human spirit involved both policy
and practice. Rarely were these children believed when they
tried to inform authorities of their plight. Yet the stolen
children survived — and so did stories of their relentless
resistance.

Five generations of my family have been affected by
removal of children. Four generations of my family
have been removed from their mothers and
institutionalised. Three generations of my family have
been put into Beagle Bay Mission dormitories. Four
generations of my family went without parently love,
without mother or father. I myself found it very hard to
show any love to my children because I wasn't given
that, so was my mother and grandmother.
When I think back on my childhood days — we
should have been treated better than we were by the
Church. We were mistreated badly, I was abused by the
missionaries from all angles — sexual, physical and
mental. I am a strong person in myself. I had to be
strong, I had no-one to turn to, no-one to guide me
through life. (Bird 1998, 65–66)

A striking feature of these stories is that, in spite of the
confusion, emptiness, sadness and suffering, these children
found ways to survive and resist their oppressors. The spirits
of these young people were never completely crushed. They
survive in this land as people who have known some of the
worst abuses that humans can inflict on each other. They
survive as testimony to the sin of assimilation, attempts to
erase identity and crush lives — often in the name of religion

and even in the name of Jesus Christ. They survive as a living symbol of tragic suffering at the heart of the Australian community. They are part of this community, and part of who we now are; knowing their story is now part of being Australian.

The stolen children are a powerful Australian symbol of tragic suffering, courageous survival and compassionate spirit. They represent those Aboriginal children who, once stolen, now give life to others; once denied identity, they now enhance the identity of Australians; once wounded, they now heal Australians who feel the shame of Australia's past.

In an earlier chapter I outlined seven representative suffering sites throughout Australia. These are sites where massacres have occurred, where waterholes have been poisoned or where Aborigines have been flogged. They are also sites where Aboriginal Australians resisted, struggled and survived despite the odds. Aboriginal blood still cries out from the land at these sites. Yet the stories from most of these sites are all too easily dismissed as vague memories of the distant past that do not stir our souls or move non-indigenous peoples to compassion. They do not touch our immediate lives. Stories of troopers killing Aboriginal people in cold blood have not moved non-Aboriginal Australians as much as these personal stories of children 'stolen' from their parents in even colder blood. Past massacres under British rule were all too easily dismissed as 'the way things were in the early days'.

The story of suffering experienced by the stolen children, however, is somehow different. It has moved many Australians who would otherwise remain aloof. The living voices of these children have struck chords of shame and compassion in the consciences of many Australian communities. It is hard for me to believe that Australians, who pride themselves in human rights and giving people 'a fair go', could behave so callously towards indigenous children. These stories make us feel ashamed to be Australian.

A symbol of healing

Why did this group of Aboriginal people suffer? Is there more to this suffering than a tragic accident of history? One way of answering these questions is to follow the cue of Veronica Brady quoted at the head of this chapter, and speak of this group of indigenous Australians as 'suffering servants'. Brady is referring to a biblical precedent — a symbol of healing I would now like to explore.

How is this stolen generation like the suffering servant mentioned in Brady's quote from the prophet Isaiah? The fact that many of the stolen generation spoke of themselves as 'slaves', and were in fact 'servants' of non-Aboriginal families, is both ironic and poignant. One woman fostered into a Christian family told me 'I was only permitted to enter their presence when they rang the bell'. Are these servants who suffered in Australia a 'suffering servant' in the biblical sense? Here I follow the lead of Soelle as she reads the history of those who suffered in El Salvador.

> God is moving through Central America. In the hymns
> of Isaiah the humiliated and scorned one emerges. He
> was interpreted as the Messiah, as a prophet or as the
> people. Even if the people don't know it, they are this
> suffering servant of God; they are light for us all.
> (Soelle 1995, p. 70)

There are three dimensions of the suffering servant symbol of Isaiah that invite instructive comparison.

First, the suffering servant was an individual or more probably a group among the Israelites who was oppressed, despised and crushed by the rest of the people — possibly at the time of their exile into Babylon. The symbol remains ambiguous; the precise identification of the original suffering servant remains open. I need only quote a few of the lines from Isaiah 53 to illustrate the similarities between the

original suffering community in Israel and the suffering
stolen children in Australia.

> He had no form or majesty that we should look at him,
> nothing in his appearance that we should desire him.
> He was despised and rejected by others;
> a man of suffering and acquainted with infirmity;
> as one from whom others hide their faces
> he was despised and we held him of no account.
> (Isaiah 53:2–3)

> He was oppressed and he was afflicted,
> yet he did not open his mouth;
> like a lamb that is led to the slaughter,
> and like a sheep that before its shearers is silent,
> so he did not open his mouth.
> By a perversion of justice he was taken away.
> Who could have imagined his future? (Isaiah 53:7–8)

The point of this comparison is not to discern an exact
correspondence as if this text were a prediction, but to
indicate that this symbol is open: other figures or groups can
be discerned fulfilling a similar function in God's plan of
reconciliation. The suffering servant is a corporate symbol of
the suffering remnant of Israel; the stolen generation as a
symbol points to a suffering remnant in Australian history.
The stolen children are a remnant that testifies to the
rejection and oppression of all those people chosen by the
Spirit of the Land to be the original custodians of this land,
people taken away from their own place by a 'perversion of
justice'. The stolen children are the symbol of the suffering
remnant: Aboriginal people who have survived the holocaust
of colonialisation.

Second, the suffering of this servant figure is more than
the suffering of daily life; this suffering is in some way
redemptive, vicarious and mediated to all God's people. The
stolen children represent a comparable symbol of 'healing'

for Australia; they were generally regarded as rejects, afflicted with the curse of being 'half-castes', or 'inferior creatures'. Even more, they were bruised by police beatings, afflicted by European diseases, and 'crushed by our iniquities'. Yet many immigrant Australians saw the stricken condition of the stolen children as the very work of God: some 'races' were weak and inferior as part of God's plan.

The stories of suffering experienced by the children and parents of the stolen generation have had a remarkable effect on many Australians. These stories, more than all the accounts of massacres, have moved many communities to acknowledge their past, the shame of their history and their sins. The people behind these stories have confronted the Australian public with the genuine human face, heart and soul of the Aboriginal people, not the racist stereotypes many had come to believe. The living voices of the stolen children, perhaps more than those of any other group, have helped many to overcome the barrier between Aboriginal and non-Aboriginal Australians. These indigenous Australians have moved the process of reconciliation forward, and given renewed hope to many. In short, their stories have been a healing force within the Australian community; the stolen children have become a symbol of reconciliation.

While the current Australian government has not — at the time of writing this text — issued a formal apology for the policy and practices which led to the stolen generation, a number of church bodies have responded with empathetic apologies. These apologies are not only a recognition of the wrongs committed against these children, but also indications that the story of the suffering has encouraged renewed participation in the reconciliation process. I see these apologies as a sign that the stolen generation has functioned as a healing symbol like the suffering servant, helping to overcome the alienation between indigenous and non-indigenous Australians. I believe this remains true, even though in terms of justice, the funds allocated by the

Howard government in November 1997 to address the grievances outlined in the so-called stolen-generation report, are totally inadequate.

In many contexts, one of the remarkable characteristics of the stolen children is the generous spirit exhibited by many of those who experienced the deprivation of their human rights in missions, homes and institutions — the suffering sites of the period. These people are now seeking reconciliation not revenge. These people are now extending forgiveness not disgust. These people are now expressing love not hate. More specifically, the act of forgiveness and acceptance extended by the stolen children so violently 'afflicted' helps to heal us, helps to make us whole, helps to reconcile Aboriginal and non-Aboriginal peoples in this land. Or, to paraphrase Isaiah, 'by their tears we are healed'.

Third, one of the significant reasons why the 'suffering servant' traditionally served as a significant symbol of reconciliation is that people identified with the symbol. They owned it. They felt a connection, a common bond. They were united by their connection with the suffering servant. Both indigenous and non-indigenous Australians identify with the stolen children. These children are becoming a healing symbol with which both parties — Aboriginal and non-Aboriginal — can connect. They suffered, yet through the story of their suffering, the barriers to reconciliation are being broken down.

The stories of the stolen children are an integral part of Australian history, a part of our common history as Australians — even if it is painful. In our local communities, I believe we must connect with the suffering of the stolen generation as a powerful human reality in our midst. In our search for Australia's soul, I believe we can also connect with this generation in a moral and spiritual way. A potential spiritual bond is present if we can but grasp it. When we do, then the stolen generation is a national tragedy that can help unite and reconcile the alienated peoples of Australia.

The suffering Spirit

In chapter 5 I reflected, as many have done, on the Spirit of the Land experienced by indigenous Australians as a creative force forming this land and establishing its Law. Christians, both Aboriginal and non-Aboriginal, have associated this Spirit of the Land with the Creator Spirit or God the Creator. In chapter 6 I considered the suffering land as integral to the spirituality of Aboriginal peoples in Australia. A related spiritual reality, which has not been given as much attention, is Aboriginal experience of the suffering Spirit. Galarrwuy Yunupingu says, you 'experience the suffering of the Spirit of the Land because of the carelessness of the non-Aboriginal people who call themselves "owners" of this land' (Yunupingu 1996, p. 10).

When the land suffers, when the stolen children suffer, when families suffer dispossession or destruction, the Spirit of the Land suffers. The suffering of the Spirit of the Land deep within this land is expressed forcefully in *Rainbow Spirit Theology*. The Rainbow Spirit Elders speak of the Spirit of the Land, called the Creator Spirit in their text, crying with the land and the people because the deep spiritual bonds between the land and its people have been broken; because the sacred places of the land have been desecrated; because the land has been dispossessed; because the life forces formed in the land have been destroyed; because the blood of Aboriginal people has been spilled; and because those bonds which linked people to the land and sustained family structures have been broken (Rainbow Spirit Elders 1997, pp 42–54).

The Spirit of the Land who created the Aboriginal people and their culture has not abandoned them and retired into heaven, history, or the earth. The suffering goes on — in the Spirit of the Land suffering with the land and the people of the land. And where the Spirit suffers there is compassion, there is hope, there is a spiritual force at work for reconciliation that transcends our human efforts. Where the Spirit of the Land suffers there is potential for new life in the land. I see the survival story of the stolen children as part of the healing work of a suffering God present in our land. The suffering Spirit of the Land is the suffering God in the indigenous experience of Aboriginal people.

I may be amazed at the grandeur of Kakadu, the mystery of Uluru, the magic of the rain forest, and sense the presence of the Creator in these glories of creation. The majesty of the cosmos, however, is like a beautiful mask that hides the God behind the mask: the God in pain, the God of compassion, the suffering Spirit. I know this God because I know the cross. The cross reveals to me the compassion of God for all oppressed peoples; ultimately the holiness or otherness of God is not found in power, but in pathos.

The cross is the symbol that points me back to the stolen children as a symbol of the Spirit's presence in Australia's history. The cross, for me, is not an abstract philosophical symbol. The cross points to a God who lived and died as Jesus Christ in real space and time. The cross means the spiritual was — and is — present in the mess of history, including Australian history.

The cross is not a symbol of might or majesty; the cross was — and is — a symbol of injustice and disgrace. God chose to associate with this symbol of suffering, a symbol with which suffering humans are also challenged to identify. The stolen children are a symbol of injustice and disgrace with which this suffering God now associates. By connecting with the cross through my faith, I believe I received forgiveness for my personal sins. By extension I could preach to the oppressed of society — whether they be the stolen generation or the martyrs of San Salvador — and assure them that by faith in Christ, their individual sins are forgiven. The problem, however, is not the sins that these oppressed people may have committed personally. The problem is the corporate sins of their society that cause oppression and dehumanisation. The problem is the corporate sins committed against indigenous Australians. The crisis for oppressed communities is not their own sins but the sins of others — the sins that cause their suffering. Where is Christ in their sufferings — their unjust sufferings caused by structural, corporate or social sin? Where is God when they reach out to their oppressors in search of justice and reconciliation?

According to the elders in *Rainbow Spirit Theology*,

> Christ who suffered on the cross continues to suffer
> with the land and the people of the land. In the
> suffering of the land and the people of the land, we see
> Christ suffering and we hear Christ crying out.
> (Rainbow Spirit Elders 1997, p. 67)

According to Moltmann, the power of the cross is reflected in Elie Wiesel's story of God's humiliation in Auschwitz.

> The SS hanged two Jewish men and a youth in front of
> the whole camp. The men died quickly, but the death
> throes of the youth lasted for half an hour. 'Where is
> God? Where is he?' someone asked behind me. As the
> youth hung in torment in the noose after a long time,
> I heard the man call again, 'Where is God now?' And
> I heard a voice in myself answer, 'Where is he? He is
> here. He is hanging there on the gallows . . .'
> (Moltmann 1974, p. 273)

The suffering or pathos of God present in Auschwitz continues in Australia. The shame of the cross is relived by God every day of every year where human beings suffer injustice. God not only suffers with the oppressed, but 'in, with and under' them. God suffered in the suffering servant. In Australia, God suffers as the Spirit of the Land present in the stolen generation — and all other generations of Aboriginal people who suffered and died for this land.

The stolen children are indeed a powerful symbol of tragic suffering, courageous survival and compassionate spirit. This symbol is one with which indigenous and many non-indigenous Australians identify today. Both parties are brought together by this symbol — a symbol that points immediately to the suffering Spirit of the Land, and ultimately to the suffering God of the cross, as a deep healing power working in the reconciliation process.

The search

Not only those of us who use the cross as a lens to read history may discern the presence of the suffering God in the stolen generation. Those sensitive to the soul, the spirit, the mystery of Australia will sense the deep connections between the story of the stolen children and the pathos of our history. There is more to the story of the stolen generation than a sad tale. The presence and the pain of God, the Spirit of God lamenting in this land, calls to us from just below the surface.

If we, as indigenous and non-indigenous Australians, acknowledge our connection with the stolen generation, we have a common symbol that binds us together. We can be united around a common symbol of suffering, resistance and healing. We can each respect our past identity and culture. The tears of the stolen generation link us as people in pain, Australians in pain. The symbol of the stolen children draws us together to reflect on the mystery of the Spirit working through this suffering people to effect reconciliation within this land. The forgiving words of the stolen children reflects the Spirit of the Land at work healing those who feel the shame of this symbol. In short, the pathos of the stolen generation becomes part of our collective soul as Australians.

This symbol, I believe, points to a spiritual dimension in the Australian soul that many in the pub, in the office and around the barbecue may deny — or perhaps hide. That spiritual dimension is more than a sense of the sacred in the red centre, more than the energy of Australia competing as an isolated island against the rest of the world. The spiritual is in the story of the suffering and resisting survival of the indigenous peoples of this land. The spiritual is the Spirit of the Land suffering in the stolen children and with other stolen, brutalised and almost destroyed indigenous Australians. The very presence of those who resisted, survived and reached out to forgive is testimony to the spiritual, the soul of this land.

CHAPTER 9

BEING AUSTRALIAN

The genuine 'Australia' is not there simply to be
proclaimed or packaged as an image for the tourist
industry. It still has to be formed. (Kelly 1990, p. 39)

My pilgrimage

I am Australian. I love this wide brown land — its soil, its
songs, its stories, its spirit. I have stood in the wake of a
bushfire with a vision of ashes in all directions: black where
once was brown, where once was green.

I have tasted yabbies fresh from the dam, swallowed dust
that once was soil, heard the scratching of possums on the
tin roof and celebrated when the late summer rains hit the
dry stubble. I have wandered through the bush in search of
rabbits, those British pests that pockmark the landscape and
displace the cheeky bandicoot.

I have sat on the floor beside my mother's feet as she
pumped the pedals of an organ to create music in a bush
church. I have sat beneath a peppercorn tree chasing the
magpies from the apricots my grandmother was drying in the
summer sun.

I have stood still at dawn as the light turned night into monument and old men into diggers, lost in memory with mates from a distant war — and I have wondered why they made such a sacrifice for this land. I have driven an FJ Holden and owned a Kingswood. I enjoy 'Waltzing Matilda', and I recall as a boy, during the Depression, 'swaggies' who walked the roads hoping for a meal in exchange for chopping a load of firewood.

As a young man I left my land for some years only to return in search of scenes etched on my psyche, landscapes of my identity — more than the images that commercial artists project as icons of who we are as Australians: Uluru or the bridge in Sydney. I was searching for more than gleaming beaches and ghost gums, though these too are etched on my inner landscape, my inscape. I was seeking more than glossy brochures could offer.

Since returning to Australia in 1974 I have been searching for the soul of Australia, searching the landscape, the story and the people for the inscape of Australia. Did artists such as McCubbin or Namatjira capture the soul of Australia? Do poets such as Judith Wright or Mudrooroo? Were the images etched on my inscape adequate to describe the face of Australia's identity? Or were some colours and contours missing?

In the silence of the scrub I could sense the Spirit of the Land, even if I kept my feelings to myself. In the paths of the pioneers, like my great-grandparents, I could feel the faith that drove them to create a rustic new world. In the dreams of the explorers I could glimpse the hope of a people striving to belong. But then, quite suddenly, I would find myself enclosed within the four walls of a church building — and within a European faith transplanted in text and architecture.

I have lived the ambiguity of being Australian, a rural youth incarnate in an adult religious academic seeking a spiritual centre beyond my city balcony, my 'Aussie verandah' where questions of meaning are posed (Pickard 1998, p. 5).

Should my verandah be facing inward to the red hot heart? Or outward to coasts and colonial conquests? Or back to sights and sounds suppressed?

At different times I think perhaps all three may be necessary to capture the substance of being Australian; in the present struggle for reconciliation, I believe I must follow the third course. The way to the soul of Australia, it seems to me, is a pilgrimage back through the landscape, through the stories, through suppressed memories to sites of resistance and suffering, the silent sacred places in Australia's history. In the chapters of this book I have begun that journey.

I may wish to escape this pilgrimage and move forward aided by bouts of amnesia. I may wish to glimpse a vision of the future soul of Australia, rampant like a boxing kangaroo on the flag at my helm. I may anticipate national glory in media or business while ignoring a festering heritage of injustice caused by two centuries of that poison called racism. I may dream of a mature country transcending the 'shadow' of Britain, and celebrating Australia's identity as an equal player on the world stage — at least in sporting events.

Something of what I feel as I began this pilgrimage — along with many other advocates of reconciliation — is expressed by New Zealand poet James Baxter.

> The corpses of Hamburg. The corpses of Vietnam. By a massive displacement of conscience we do not have to bear the weight of them. We antipodeans are an innocent people. Yet I think our peculiar absence of guilt may be a heavier burden to carry than the guilt itself.
>
> There are those other corpses that lie under our fat green fields. The corpses of the [Maori] Land Wars ... Our forgetting is too like amnesia. I think the god of death takes charge of us in spite of our innocence. We are unable to wholly opt out of history. By a process like osmosis, like the seeping of water through gravel,

the calamities in which we have not participated reach
into our dreams. (Baxter 1971, p. 8)

I too believe that the calamities from Australia's past —
and many other stories — reach into my dreams. In recent
years those stories have surfaced in our national
consciousness as moral forces in the reconciliation process.
My pilgrimage is no longer back to my roots in Europe,
where I can relish my own family history, but to those sites
of Australian history where 'the calamities in which we have
not participated' haunt my dreams — and my conscience.

My pilgrimage is a search for Australia's soul, the
spiritual that persists in the story of Australia. My pilgrimage
differs from that identified by Manning Clark who states the
following is one of his aims in 'telling the story' of Australia.

My purpose was also to show how human beings
responded to the decline of faiths which had comforted
human beings for thousands of years, and to portray
the pilgrimage of man [sic] from the Kingdom of God
to the Kingdom of Nothingness. (Clark 1976, p. 52)

Making connections

For me to be Australian in the context of reconciliation is to
explore this land anew, with a second naiveté; not conquering
but uncovering, not emulating European explorers with
nameless Aboriginal guides, but searching as a student of the
Spirit who permeates the Australian landscape and its stories.
The focus of my search is not so much the topography of the
land but its epigraphy — not the terrifying red desert
imprinted on my psyche, but the bold stories written on the
landscape that connect me with the inscape of Australia.

Honouring the dead

The Anzac legend is only part of the story of how Australia's
identity was 'formed'. Men and women bravely went to war

in battlefields far from home to defend Australia. Many of them paid the supreme sacrifice: they 'gave their lives' for this land. They followed in the wake of the Anzacs whose tenacity against great odds 'put Australia on the map' and helped form Australia's identity. The names of those who died for this land in these wars are remembered on monuments in almost every town across the country — and rightly so.

Not so the Aboriginal heroes who also gave their lives for this land. If I visit the many suffering sites in this land — some of which are described in an earlier chapter — I find numerous stories about the indigenous dead. But there are no names, no monuments, and no honour. Yet at each of these sites indigenous people fought for their country and gave their lives for this land. They were the custodians of this land, and they lived — and died — to preserve this land. Some may find it meaningful to return to the battlefields of Normandy or Gallipoli. I believe it is time to visit the 'battlefields of Australia', the sites of resistance and suffering where Aboriginal people 'paid the supreme sacrifice'.

Let me begin at the centre of this new world, the *axus mundi*: Uluru, the rock where the 'dreaming tracks' meet and tourists gaze in wonder. The dark side of the centre is the massacre at Coniston, a site no one visits to honour the indigenous dead. Here, in the centre of this land, the last recorded massacre in Australia took place. Ironically, the man who led the massacre was an Anzac veteran. This final massacre represents for me the many Aboriginal lives given for this land and never remembered. Their sacrifice has formed our identity as much as the sacrifice of those who fought abroad.

The 'storylines' of massacres around the country are trails of blood that meet in the red centre, the site of the last massacre. To be Australian is not only to hail the rock as the sacred centre, but also to acknowledge the blood of those whose lives were shed so other immigrant Australians could enjoy this land. Uluru is indeed a symbol of Australia's soul — and a monument to her living indigenous dead.

For me, to be Australian, then, is to embrace these sites of suffering and resistance as integral to my Australian identity. These places, from Sydney Cove to Colebrook Home, have become sacred sites where I now see more than tragedy. These sites, alongside many others, are sacred places, where the interaction of indigenous and immigrant Australians is crucial. I use the word crucial deliberately because the word derives from *crux*, cross, and points to these places as locations of critical interaction. These locations can, of course, be seen as blots on the Australian character, symbols of shame.

They can also be identified as sites marked by unseen indigenous crosses, places where Aboriginal people resisted, suffered and died for Australia, for this land and its future. I believe it is time to honour the indigenous dead as lives sacrificed for this land. They are integral to Australia's identity — they still haunt her soul.

Embracing the other

Reconciliation means embracing Aboriginal peoples as an integral feature of our Australian inscape. Embracing demands more than tolerating, accepting or acknowledging Aboriginal presence. Embracing requires more than ruling, as the High Court did in 1992, that this land was not *terra nullius*, but inhabited with Aboriginal peoples. Embracing extends beyond celebrating Aboriginal arts, music and mystery as exotic additions to our cultural displays. Embracing as an act of reconciliation means embracing the other party as 'other'; it means respecting and celebrating the difference. The history of Australian policy has been to reject the other as 'pagan' and 'savage'; to trivialise the other as 'uncivilised' and 'simple-minded'; to ignore the other as 'worthless' and 'near extinction'; or to assimilate the other into the 'white race'. Rarely, if ever, did any Australian policy or practice treat the 'other', the Aborigine, as equal in value or significance to 'civilised Australians'. The poison of racism blinded non-indigenous Australians to the 'otherness' of Aboriginal people as significant and integral to Australia's identity. Conversely, the 'otherness' of the non-indigenous invaders held little appeal to indigenous peoples forced to live as 'civilised' Europeans.

In earlier chapters I have outlined some of the profound features of Aboriginal culture to be appreciated as 'other', distinctively different from non-Aboriginal cultures yet deeply spiritual and inherently ecological. Aboriginal cultures can boast sophisticated systems of indigenous Law which integrate society, religion and the environment. This Law is the 'natural' law of the land, and part of Australia's total identity.

Perhaps the most fascinating and controversial feature of Aboriginal culture as 'other' is its spiritual world. In the past, some dismissed Aboriginal spirituality as fertility religion and 'the work of the devil'. Others classified it neatly as a type of primal, tribal or primitive religion of academic interest but not relevant to Australia's identity. Still others explored similarities between indigenous and biblical spiritualities.

Valuing the 'other' of Aboriginal spirituality demands, I would argue, that Aboriginal experiences of the Spirit are accepted as being as significant as those of other peoples, be they biblical or European. Christian experiences of the Spirit are quite diverse but can still perhaps all be symbolised by the expressions 'Holy Spirit' or 'Jesus Christ'. To indicate that the Aboriginal experience of the Spirit is 'other' than European experience, yet a significant experience to be valued, I have followed the lead of a number of Aboriginal writers and used the term 'Spirit of the Land' as a symbol to express this experience. The spiritual dimension of the Australian soul is more than the residue of immigrant readings of the Spirit's presence in the landscape, or explicitly Christian readings of the Spirit's presence in Word and Sacrament. Australia's soul also embraces indigenous experiences of the Spirit of the Land — the spiritual that is integral to this land and its original custodians.

To embrace the 'other' means to understand, value and make meaningful connections with Aboriginal cultures, including their spiritual centre, but without seeking to appropriate or exploit the 'other'. I am not suggesting that immigrant Australians are looking to Aborigines with 'tremendous envy and spiritual longing', to transform their inner lives. I am not looking to Aboriginal peoples to be the shamans who lead immigrant Australians out of a spiritual malaise.

Nor am I seeking to appropriate Aboriginal spirituality as the new entrée into the Australian psyche because, as Stanner said, 'White man got no Dreaming' (Tacey 1995, p. 133). Rather, I am advocating that immigrant Australians explore, value and make connections where appropriate with Aboriginal culture and embrace these 'other' experiences as part of who we all are as Australians. The indigenous 'other' is a part of Australia's soul.

Feeling the pathos

For me to be Australian at this deeper level I need to embrace even the 'deaths of the other' as points where I seek to identify — in some sacred way — with the indigenous oppressed rather than the non-indigenous oppressors. My goal is not a kind of cultural appropriation even of the dead, but a journey from shame to sorrow, from personal *Angst* to suffering with the sufferer. My hope is that I might know — vicariously in some small measure as a human being — the pathos of Aboriginal history so that I may not be alienated from my Australian soul for ever.

Knowing the pathos of another involves hearing the stories of suffering and resistance from the sites of suffering and resistance in this land — or, rather, re-living these stories through storytellers, mediators of the Spirit of the Land hidden in the stories.

In rituals of healing, like the one performed at *The Fountain of Tears* in Adelaide on Sorry Day 1998, a group of non-indigenous Australians said sorry and confessed our shame over the treatment of the stolen children. We also began to identify with the sorrow, the tears, the pathos of the stolen generation.

By identifying with that living symbol I discerned another dimension of the Australian soul. Those indigenous Australians present who had suffered told their story, and then listened to our communal apology. They accepted our apology and forgave us. Among the survivors of the sins committed by immigrant Australians, there was a spiritual power to heal. They were mediators of the healing Spirit among us.

This act of forgiveness reveals a generous spirit, a deep grace that dwells within Aboriginal survivors and rises up to touch empathetic listeners. This gift begins the healing process and initiates a spiritual bonding — through suffering, through resisting the oppression, and through breaking down the barriers — that facilitates authentic reconciliation.

The suggested healing rites offer options for re-telling the events at sites of suffering and resistance, feeling the pathos, sensing the sacred, and experiencing the healing of both social and spiritual shame. These rites can be adapted to the spiritual orientation of a given community so that a meaningful connection between each tradition and the Spirit of the Land is celebrated.

The experience of the spiritual has been different for Aboriginal people and immigrant Australians. Aboriginal people have known the Spirit of the Land creating life in the land for thousands of years. They have also known the Spirit that has sustained them through the last 200 years of suffering. For me, while the experience may differ, the suffering Spirit of indigenous Australia is the suffering God of my heritage — but with a different face. In rites of healing at these sites I believe indigenous and non-indigenous Australians can find in the pathos of the suffering Spirit a symbol that can bind Aboriginal and non-Aboriginal, a symbol of Australia's soul.

It is difficult to bond across a bargaining table, on a parliamentary floor, in a battlefield, or at a political meeting. A bonding that reflects genuine reconciliation will only come when we, as immigrant Australians, willingly hear the story of a site of suffering and resistance, experience something of the pathos, confess our shame and our pain, celebrate rites of healing, and join together in a common struggle for justice.

Joining the struggle

The vision of reconciliation can easily be blurred. Urgent political agendas, economic pressures, frantic developments in information technology, and the excitement of a new millennium can easily distract Australians from pursuing the struggle for justice and reconciliation. During the recent 1998 election campaign neither of the major parties seriously introduced reconciliation as central to their vision for Australia. With the amendment to the Wik legislation passed by the Howard government, politicians seemed to be happy to see the so-called 'race issue' disappear, even if that legislation limited Aboriginal people's right to negotiate land settlements and probably set the course of reconciliation back many years.

The vision of reconciliation demands, I believe, a nation whose soul is open enough to embrace more than economic values and political compromise. It is a vision of people — both indigenous and non-indigenous — who hold this land as sacred, and an integral part of their identity. It is a vision of people — both indigenous and non-indigenous — who do not sever their ties with a common history of invasion, dispossession and survival.

The vision of reconciliation is more than a vague dream about all Australians being 'happy little egalitarians'. This vision is one of social justice for Aboriginal people in every aspect of Australian life — a vision of human respect and equal rights. It is not the agenda of this book to delineate the many injustices that Aboriginal people still experience. Suffice it to say that popular cries that 'too much money has been thrown at Aboriginal people', that 'Aboriginal people have got too much land already,' or that 'nothing has got better, so why throw good money after bad,' are unfounded and unfair (ATSIC 1998, pp. 13–21).

The vision of reconciliation ought not to remain the province of ATSIC, the Council for Aboriginal Reconciliation, and a few Aboriginal activists. Reconciliation is a profound moral, social and spiritual process that touches all of us and offers to enrich our identity. This vision is a call for people in every community to become informed advocates. As such, they become advocates of 'forming' Australia with values that uphold the traditional principles of a 'fair go for all', and 'defending the underdog', as deep moral values that ought also to apply to the indigenous peoples.

The vision of reconciliation means getting involved in the struggle for justice, raising consciousness, changing attitudes, and performing rites of healing at the local level. Organisations such as ANTAR (Australians for Native Title and Reconciliation) offer excellent opportunities for local people to become advocates of reconciliation.

One place where I believe each of us should be advocates for change in particular is in Australian schools. All children need a deep sense of what it means to be Australian — socially, morally and spiritually. As Linda Burney writes,

> [my] vision for all young people going through the school system in this country is that Aboriginal Studies will be a mandatory part of every child's experience, and that it should be as normal as History or English. This needs to be a fundamental part of developing the Australian identity. (ATSIC 1998, p. 37)

I also support the vision of a document on reconciliation, provided that such a document is more than a convenient political exercise timed to coincide with the centenary of Federation in 2001. This document would need to incorporate a genuine recognition of the social, moral and spiritual factors explored in the preceding chapters of this book — even if the process takes many years to achieve, as has been the case in other countries (such as New Zealand). This document would need to be committed to social justice, equal rights and reparation for past injustices.

This document would also need to be developed with full consultation and negotiation with the Aboriginal people — in contrast to what happened with the amendments to the Wik legislation in 1998. Only then would this document begin to redress the injustice first perpetrated by James Cook in 1770, when he breached the imperial government's explicit instructions by claiming the East Coast of Australia for Britain. 'You are also with the Consent of the Natives [*sic*] to take possession of Convenient Situations in the Country and in the Name of King of Gt Britain' (Council 1994a, 165).

After the pilgrimage

I am Australian. I live in a sacred land with sacred sites, sacred trails and sacred stories etched into the landscape from deep in primordial time. I belong to a land of golden soil kept fertile by centuries of indigenous custodians, kin to the land and all its inhabitants, and in tune with its soul. I dwell in a mysterious land where the spiritual — the Spirit of the Land — once experienced as the ongoing source of indigenous life and culture, reaches into my present.

I live in a conquered land with suffering sites, trails of explorers and brutal stories etched on the landscape where indigenous people resisted and indigenous blood was shed. I belong to a land where pioneer men and women fought the odds to establish a frontier colony, and where Anzac men and women fought the foe to establish a frontier identity. Yet I dwell in a land where racism led to policies and acts of brutality against indigenous men and women, acts of which I am ashamed. I live in a land where the shameful events of the past have been hidden and suppressed.

I live in an affluent land with vast spaces dedicated to sheep, deep mines devoted to discovering all kinds of 'gold', and cities sprawled along the coastline. I live in an aggressive place that sends forth ambassadors from its verandah to win glory in all kinds of foreign games. I live in a broken land where the indigenous custodians who survived dispossession and near genocide confront me with the pathos of their past and their present, a pathos that informs their resilient vision of reconciliation, and their remarkable willingness to forgive.

I have found within this land something far more powerful than the 'conquest of desert' by explorers or the 'conquest of the bush' by pastoralists. I have found an indigenous people, whose desert lands and bush homes have been conquered and crushed by immigrant Australians, yet who have a generosity of spirit that reflects the Spirit of the Land. They resisted genocide, yet they are ready to forgive — and forgive again — in the hope of reconciliation and healing. I have found a deep underlying compassion at the heart of this land.

I knew the Spirit of God through the story of the cross, the story of a suffering God in human flesh and human history. I now realise that this Spirit has been experienced in a radically different way by the indigenous people of the land as the Spirit of the Land. I no longer relate to the Creator exclusively with the images and symbols inherited from European Christianity. I can now reach out to the Spirit within this land — not only in the landscape but in the history of suffering and resistance in this land.

I am Australian. I am moved by the symbols that reveal the spiritual at the heart of this land. The rock — the symbol of the centre, the place of sacred power but also the place of historical shame — an indigenous Golgotha. The stolen children — the symbol of human suffering, indigenous pathos and deep healing, the symbol with whom many non-indigenous Australians now identify — an indigenous suffering servant. The land — the symbol of the Spirit of the Land, a deep creative presence experienced for many centuries and a profound suffering presence experienced since colonialisation — an indigenous holy land. The cross — the symbol of a suffering God known to Christians as the ultimate power behind all reconciliation. For me, all these spiritual forces are integrated in the soul that is Australia's.

APPENDIX

HEALING RITES AT SEVEN SITES

The task of deep remembering calls for new schools, for
ways of learning from each other across ethnic, racial and
cultural divides. It calls for forms of sharing that
deliberately transcend accustomed patterns of academic
exchange and seeks to build bridges between the hearts.
(Mueller-Fahrenholz 1997, p. 67)

*In chapter 3 I identified seven sites that are representative of
the suffering of the Aboriginal peoples and the sins of their
non-Aboriginal oppressors. In this chapter I present a series
of rites located symbolically at these sites as a way of
remembering the events and their significance. The goal of
these rites is to provide a potential vehicle for healing the
memories and wounds associated with these suffering sites.*

Healing rites

Healing is a vital part of the reconciliation process. We need
more than speeches and rhetoric, more than documents and

monuments, more than songs and sermons. We need to come together — indigenous and immigrant peoples — and join in rites of deep remembering that touch our souls. We need to find ways to express our sorrow, our pain and our hopes — find connecting symbols that bring us together. We need to find rites that will heal the wounds in our Australian soul.

I have structured a healing rite that makes three connections at each stage. The first connection is to link up with sites of suffering where painful encounters between indigenous and non-indigenous Australians have taken place. These are not traditional sacred sites as such. Some of them — like the Fountain of Tears in Adelaide — are already becoming 'sacred places'. In the ritual at these sites, participants may move into another time and place — as many Catholics do when following the Stations of the Cross.

The second connection is with the words — and the story — of the suffering Christ on the cross as told in the Christian Scriptures.

The third connection links this story and the story of what happened to indigenous peoples and the land at each of the seven sites. By making these associations, the pain of each remembrance may become more powerful, and increase the potential for healing.

The order of the rites follows, rather roughly, the sequence of Australian history rather than the probable order in which the words from the cross were uttered. Between each of the rites, the participants may move in reflective silence from one symbolic site to another, or sing an appropriate song as they walk to the next place of ritual remembering.

Rites of healing are powerful but rare. Powerful rites assume forms consistent with the culture where they are performed. In Australia, we have rarely performed such rites outside religious communities. Parliament does not seem to be the appropriate place for sacred observances. The following rites of healing are grounded in traditions that are meaningful to many Australians. Those who belong to the Christian faith may wish to emphasise more strongly the healing function of the cross of Christ. Those who belong to other faiths may wish to appropriate healing symbols and rites from their own tradition and adapt them. In either case, the suffering God among us provides the hidden power of healing we experience when we unite in these rites of remembrance and healing.

The rites which follow may be used in several ways. Ideally they would be performed as a totality on a day such as Good Friday, a national Healing Day, or a cultural day such as 21 October, when the Battle of Battle Mountain is commemorated in Queensland. The seven rites could be included in a sequence of Sundays in Lent. Young people in high school may wish to dramatise the text in assemblies. Local communities are invited to explore stories of injustice to the indigenous Australians in their local area, and prepare alternatives to one or more of the seven stories associated with the sites that follow. Some may wish to select one or two rites and expand them in a way that is meaningful in their communities. It is appropriate to ask local Aboriginal elders to perform a smoking ceremony at the end of a given ritual or the sequence of seven rites.

The background story to each of these rites is outlined and discussed in chapter 3 and should be read in preparation for this ritual. These stories can be dramatised, using the resources cited for additional information. A summary of the story is provided so that each participant can read this background information in silence before each stage in the ritual is performed. A model for an apology for the sins associated with each of the injustices committed at these seven sites is included at the end of chapter 7; an apology may also be incorporated in this ritual.

The seven sites chosen in this ritual for remembering our hidden history may be represented symbolically in a given community. A symbol may be set up at each of seven locations in a garden, in the bush, or in a building. Participants move from one symbolic location to the next as the ritual progresses. Alternatively, a given location could be re-created at one of the suffering sites on each of seven occasions. Ideally, the appropriate part of the ritual would also be performed simultaneously by seven volunteer groups at the actual historical locations while groups across Australia participate in the ritual in their own community.

Under the Southern Cross

Invitation

Leader:

We are invited today to walk the way of the Southern Cross, and visit seven sites from our history. We are invited to remember the deep suffering hidden behind the history represented by these sites. We are invited to participate in a deep remembering of our hidden past.

We are invited to hear again the words of Christ from the cross in a new context as they echo through our ancient land. We are invited to connect these painful words from the Christian tradition with the cries of agony of indigenous Australians from these seven Australian sites. We are invited to hear these words from the cross anew as we relive our history, face the hidden stories of what happened in our past, purge the poison of racism and seek healing for the shame — and the effects — of past injustices, the wounds of which continue today.

We are invited to come together under the Southern Cross as part of the process of remembering, repentance, reconciliation and healing in our land.

Welcome

Elder:

We welcome you to this site, the site of our ancestors, the country of the (*as appropriate to each community*) people and a site we now share as Australians. Although it is painful for us, we will walk together along the way of the Southern Cross in search of understanding and healing. Come, walk the way. Relive our shared past. Remember our ancestors. Taste our tears.

Invocation

Leader: With the Spirit of the Land
People: we will walk the way of the Southern Cross together.
Leader: Under the sign of the Southern Cross
People: we will hear again the words of Christ on the Cross.
Leader: With the suffering God deep among us
People: we will seek healing and reconciliation in our land.

Site one: invasion bay

Background

As soon as Governor Phillip and his party located a suitable place to anchor in Sydney Cove, they hoisted the Union Jack, drank toasts to their patron King George III, fired volleys of musketry and gave three cheers. The entire population of the First Fleet assembled before the flag on 7 February 1988, and took formal possession of the colony.

Captain Cook and other explorers had supposedly 'earned' the land for Britain by discovering it, a privilege reserved for Europeans. We know, of course, that the Europeans were not the first to discover Australia. We know, too, that the land was not empty (*terra nullius*). Indigenous Australians had been custodians of this country for thousands of years. The action of Governor Phillip was tantamount to an invasion. Sydney Cove is, in reality, invasion bay.

Story one

(The participants for this rite gather round a British flag on a pole. A British soldier may stand at attention on one side of the flagpole and a group of Aboriginal people may be

seated on the other. Beneath the flag is a bowl of sour wine
(vinegar) and several sponges.)
Elder:
We begin our journey in Sydney Cove
where they hoisted the British flag that day,
a flag unknown to the host nation,
waiting at a respectable distance.
They hoisted the flag and stole a land
they claimed to discover
in the name of their King.
'Forget a treaty,' they said,
'There's no one here to stop us,
no one here to shake our hand and toast a treaty.
The place is empty.'
'Lift your flasks to the king!
Fire the muskets!
Hail the empire's latest acquisition!'
Terra Australis, Terra Nullius,
stolen to house a few convicts
guilty of stealing far far less.
They spurned the hosts and their hospitality,
they spurned the custodians of the land,
and claimed 'invasion bay' as their own
— as a colony for convicts.

Word one: 'I thirst.'

Reader: John 19:28–29

Response
(To be spoken slowly with a pause between each voice.)
Voice 1: They raised a sponge with sour wine to his lips.
Voice 2: They raised a flag on behalf of the empire.
Voice 1: They raised a sponge.
Voice 2: They raised a flag.
Voice 1: I thirst.

Voice 2: Raise your drinks!
Voice 1: I thirst.
Voice 2: Here's to old England!
Voice 1: I thirst.
Voice 2: Here's to the glory of the empire!
Voice 1: I thirst.
Voice 1: Drink up!
Voice 2: I thirst.

Rite one: tasting sour wine

(The leader presents a bowl of sour wine (vinegar) before the people and then dips a sponge in the vinegar and touches it to his or her lips. The people may follow suit or a representative group may perform the rite on behalf of the people with the words, 'terra nullius'.)

Leader: We put this sour wine to our lips today,
Response: to taste the hospitality spurned at invasion bay.
Leader: We put this sour wine to our lips today,
Response: to acknowledge the sorrow and loss of the host people.
Leader: We put this sour wine to our lips,
Response: to remember the deep thirst of the one who suffered on the cross.
Leader: We put this sour wine to our lips,
Response: to acknowledge the deep thirst of the indigenous people
who suffered dispossession and death under the Southern Cross.
Leader: We put this sour wine to our lips,
Response: to remember the bitter taste the words *terra nullius* still leave in the lives of indigenous Australians.

Closure:

Leader: Spirit of the Land,
People: help us remember our hidden history.
Leader: Suffering God,

People: help our tears to flow for the pain of the past.
Leader: Reconciling Spirit,
People: heal our shame and our wounds.

Site two: genocide island

(The participants are given a long black ribbon or rope. They tie the black ribbon to their arms or round their necks and form one black line or several lines. The space on which they stand in a hall or on the sand may be shaped like a map of Tasmania. A large rock or cross is located at one end.)

Background

The Black War in Tasmania reached its heights in the 1830s and resulted in near genocide. After several years of local raids and counter-attacks, Governor Arthur, in the spring of 1830, planned a joint offensive with a regiment of soldiers, police, prisoners and settlers. They formed a human chain across the settled districts of Tasmania. This human chain, known as the 'black line', moved relentlessly southwards for three weeks. Those who eluded the net were persuaded by George Robinson, a devious diplomat, to surrender. Fewer than 200 Tasmanians from the settled districts survived — they were all wounded.

The remnants of the Tasmanian people were exiled to Flinders Island in Bass Strait. The land had been cleared of 'natives'; the genocide was almost complete. Among those who survived was the famous Truganini, who came to be know as 'the last Tasmanian'. Today we know that there are several thousand descendants of indigenous Tasmanians still resisting — albeit peacefully — the total clearance of their land by the infamous black line.

Story two
Elder:
We continue our journey under the Southern Cross

by walking across the island of genocide,
the island of Tasmania.
We walk across the island, as the early settlers did —
the soldiers, prisoners and police —
in that long black line,
that long long killing line.
The black line kept moving for weeks
hunting down humans like foxes,
and driving them into the sea.
The black line cleared the land for settlers,
cleared away its custodians.
It is finished!
A remnant was left to die in exile
on another island.
There were no mounds or markers,
no names from the Aboriginal people massacred.
There are no bloodstains left
on the land,
on our hands.
Yet from the earth and the sea their blood still cries,
cries for the land,
cries for justice, remembrance and rest.
In the going down of the sun and in the morning
will we remember them?
With the last Tasmanians,
we will remember them.

Word two: *'It is finished.'*
Reader: John 19:30–37

Response
(To be spoken slowly with a pause between each voice.)
Voice 1: One of the soldiers pierced his side with a spear.
Voice 2: We have more than a 1000 guns for the job.
Voice 1: None of his bones shall be broken.
Voice 2: Shoot them and leave them for the birds.

Voice 1: They will look on the one they pierced.
Voice 2: Send the injured into exile.
Voice 1: It is finished.
Voice 2: The island is cleared.
Voice 1: It is finished.
Voice 2: Genocide has been accomplished.
Voice 1: It is finished.
Voice 2: The black line has done its job.
Voice 1: It is finished.

Rite two: the black line
(The participants move forward in one or more black lines. They drape their ribbon over a large rock or cross with the words, 'It is finished'.)
Leader: We wear this black line around our necks,
People: because we are ashamed.
Leader: We wear this black line around our necks,
People: because we regret the injustices of the past.
Leader: We are ashamed of the racism deep in our story,
People: racism that led to attempted genocide.
Leader: We regret the clearing of Aboriginal custodians,
People: we regret the abuse of land and lives in Tasmania.

Closure
Leader: Spirit of the Land,
People: help us remember our hidden history.
Leader: Suffering God,
People: help our tears to flow for the pain of the past.
Leader: Reconciling Spirit,
People: heal our shame and our wounds.

Site three: a place of exile

Background
The so-called Protector of the Aborigines was supposed to look after the interests of indigenous Australians. The idea

was that someone had to protect the Aboriginal peoples from themselves and their pagan culture. One of the policies was to gather Aboriginal groups from diverse language groups, separate them from their country, and — as it were — exile them on settlements, reserves and missions. In exile they were forbidden to practise their culture; they were allowed to speak only English.

Among the many places of exile in North Queensland, Palm Island was renowned as the place of punishment, and Hopevale was known as a mission committed to Christian education. In spite of the efforts to erase traditional cultures, many survived to some extent. The story of how one mother buried her child's afterbirth and umbilical cord in the earth so that a spiritual link with her original country could be made through the ground illustrates how seriously Aboriginal people sought to maintain a connection with their spiritual homes.

Story three

(Each participant ties a red cord around his or her waist representing an umbilical cord. If this ceremony is performed indoors, a large earthenware pot representing the earth is located in the centre of the ritual space.)
Elder:
When we enter the reaches
of far North Queensland,
we discover oppressive places of exile.
We remember Palm — or 'punishment' — Island.
Those pagans have to be protected,
the protector said,
protected from their heathen culture,
their wild ways,
themselves.
In exile they can be purified
of corrupt cultures
and transformed into civilised servants,
regimented Christians,

speaking only the King's English
and eating damper spread with fat.
That would have been that
except for the deep spiritual roots
that sustained their stories,
their links with land,
their souls.
Their spirits live
as more and more return from their exile —
they find their stories,
their home country,
their ancestors,
themselves.

Word three: *'Father, forgive.'*
Reader: Luke 23:32–34

Response
(To be spoken slowly with a pause between each voice.)
Voice 1: Two criminals were led away.
Voice 2: Two Aborigines were led away.
Voice 1: Two criminals were led away.
Voice 2: Led away to exile — to protect them.
Voice 1: Two criminals were led away.
Voice 2: To save them from their culture.
Voice 1: Father, forgive them.
Voice 2: Protector, protect them in exile.
Voice 1: Father, forgive them.
Voice 2: Missionary, save them from their culture.
Voice 1: Father, forgive them.
Voice 2: Policeman, remove the 'half-castes'.
Voice 1: Father, forgive them —
Voice 2: for they don't know what's best;
Voice 1: for they don't know what they are doing;
Voice 2: for they don't know about God;
Voice 1: for they don't know what they are doing.

Rite three: burying the cord

(The participants file forward quietly and 'bury' their red cords in the earthenware pot, if indoors, or in a hole in the earth, if outside. As they do so they say the words, 'Spirit to spirit. Life to life.')

Leader: We bind this umbilical cord to ourselves today,

People: to express our empathy with exiled Aboriginal mothers.

Leader: We bury this umbilical cord

People: to join our spirits with Aboriginal spirits in the ground.

Leader: We bury our spirits deep in the earth

People: and ask our Father to forgive us.

Leader: We bury our lives together, black and white,

People: and ask the Spirit of the Land to bring us together.

Closure

Leader: Spirit of the Land,

People: help us remember our hidden history.

Leader: Suffering God,

People: help our tears to flow for the pain of the past.

Leader: Reconciling Spirit,

People: heal our shame and our wounds.

Site four: a feeding station

Background

Most of the Aboriginal Australians who died last century were not killed in battles or massacres. They perished because white settlers cleared away the scrub where bush tucker was found. Native animal and bird life were replaced by sheep and cattle. Aborigines and farm animals competed for the same waterholes. Natural food supplies disappeared, and local Aborigines were forced to depend on rations dispensed by non-indigenous settlers, missionaries or government officials at 'feeding stations'. Those rations were mainly second-grade flour. Dispossession meant destroying the 'bread of life' which had served these custodians of life in the land for thousands of years.

This dependency on the European invaders for food made the indigenous peoples of Australia even more vulnerable. When crises arose and racism erupted, local settlers or police sometimes laced the flour with arsenic or they poisoned the waterholes. Rations were a reward for good behaviour and compliance; withholding food was a punishment for acts of resistance. These rations continued in many regions until the 1960s. Even with the best of intentions, government and mission bodies served Aboriginal people with rations that were alien to them and tantamount to poison.

Story four
(The participants are seated around an old windmill or another symbol of rural Australia. In the centre is damper made from second-grade flour and a jug of sugar water.)
Elder:
The barren broken farmlands we cross
are empty now of bandicoot and bilby,
echidna, wombat and wallaby,
once protected for food and faith.
They were kin to humans then,
living totems to celebrate
one spirit with people.
They were one with the land —
custodians of plant and animal,
sustaining life
in scrub and soak.
Now their natural kin are gone:
the wombats are replaced with sheep,
the bush tucker cleared to make way for wheat,
and clean soaks turned into muddy watering holes.
Their spirits are empty, yearning,

there is nothing to eat,
no food for their souls,
nothing —
only the flour handed out at feeding stations
by the station boss or the local cop.
Then one day, when no longer useful,
or as punishment for killing a cow
to share as food,
their flour is laced with poison.
'Take and eat', the boss cocky says,
'This is given for you'.

Word four: 'Into your hands I commend my spirit.'
Reader: Luke 22:14–19; 23:44–49

Response
(To be spoken slowly with a pause between each voice.)
Voice 1: Into your hands I commend my spirit.
Voice 2: With bread we will break their spirit.
Voice 1: Into your hands I commend my spirit.
Voice 2: With sugar we will civilise these 'brutes'.
Voice 1: Into your hands I commend my spirit.
Voice 2: Eat up, this wheat is ground for you.
Voice 1: Take and eat, this is given for you.
Voice 2: Eat up, this is sweetened for you.
Voice 1: Take and eat, this is given for you.
Voice 2: Take and eat, this is poisoned for you.
Voice 1: Do this, in remembrance of me.

Rite four: sugar water
(The leader invites the participants to eat from the damper and to drink the sugar water, deceitful substitutes for the bread and water of life. The leader hands the bread and water to each participant with the words, 'the bread of broken life' and 'the sweet water of life'.)

Leader: We eat this bread, a ration from the 'feeding station',
People: to re-live Aborigines losing the bread of life from the bush.
Leader: We drink this water, sweetened with sugar,
People: to re-live the broken promises of a better life once civilised.
Leader: We eat this bitter bread,
People: to re-live the last supper of poisoned Aborigines.
Leader: We drink this water, polluted with sugar,
People: to re-live Aboriginal deaths by 'white' means.
Leader: We eat and drink in sorrow and regret.
People: We re-live these meals to heal our shame.

Closure
Leader: Spirit of the Land,
People: help us remember our hidden history.
Leader: Suffering God,
People: help our tears to flow for the pain of the past.
Leader: Reconciling Spirit,
People: heal our shame and our wounds.

Site five: Maralinga

Background
Between 1952 and 1956 the British, with the approval of the Australian government, exploded twelve nuclear weapons in three Australian locations — on the Monte Bello Islands off the north-west coast, and at Emu and Maralinga in South Australia. The Aboriginal Australians living in the so-called 'prohibited zone' around the test sites of Emu and Maralinga were forced to leave their lands — their spiritual homes — and the sacred sites they had known for thousands of years. Many of them were taken to mission stations like Koonibba.

All life and land in these areas were contaminated; Aboriginal Australians both inside and outside the prohibited

zone were exposed to radioactive contamination and fallout.
Aborigines at Wallatinna reported a big 'black mist' coming
from the direction of Emu. This black radioactive cloud
brought sickness and death to the people. The 'red sands' of
which the people were proud became 'poisoned' and grey.
The Aboriginal people of these lands suffered more than
dislocation. They suffered dehumanisation because political
leaders were willing to sacrifice Aboriginal lives for an
alleged 'greater good'. They had their spirits crushed in a
nuclear power game. In recent years a few Aboriginal
Australians are returning to the fringes of the prohibited
zone. Their spirits are rising again.

Story five
*(The participants form a series of concentric circles around a
barren space on the ground, covered with ashes. The barren
space represents Maralinga.)*
We arrive at the dry reaches of Maralinga,
desolate and desecrated,
a God-forsaken site.
Here darkness covered the land
with a cloud of thick death.
We cross the broken fence that warns
of radioactive fallout still alive,
long after the atomic blasts of the 1950s.
We meet a few Aboriginal people
returning to the fringes of the bomb sites —
they once were sacred.
They are returning to their country.
Why?
'Because our country has missed us.'
We ask them whether their suffering
from the fallout, the forced removal,
and the desecration of their lands,
was worth the sacrifice?
After all, said the politicians,

'We need this land to test these bombs
to keep the free world free.'

Word five: *'Why have you forsaken me?'*
Reader: Luke 27:45–54

Response
(To be spoken slowly with a pause between each voice. While these voices are heard the participants cover their eyes to protect them from the atomic blast.)
Voice 1: And darkness covered the whole land.
Voice 2: An atomic device exploded in the centre.
Voice 1: And darkness covered the whole land.
Voice 2: A 'dark mist' spread from the centre.
Voice 1: And darkness covered the whole land.
Voice 2: The earth shook and rocks split.
Voice 1: And darkness covered the whole land.
Voice 2: The contaminated skies screamed,
Voice 1: why have you forsaken me?
Voice 2: The people forcibly removed cried out,
Voice 1: why have you forsaken me?
Voice 2: The deserted red sands groaned,
Voice 1: why have you forsaken me?
Voice 2: The Spirit deep in the earth moaned,
Voice 1: why have you forsaken me?
Voice 2: And darkness covered the whole land.
Voice 1: And darkness covered the whole land.

Rite five: nuclear ash
(The leader takes some of the ash and marks the forehead of each of the participants with the words, 'the mark of Maralinga'.)
Leader: We mark our foreheads with ash
People: to remember those who suffered from the fallout.
Leader: We cover this space with 'nuclear' ash

People: to remember desecrated sands and sites across Australia.
Leader: We cover our eyes with our hands
People: to remember the blinding force of desecration
and to confess our blindness to the suffering
of indigenous Australians in desecrated places.

Closure
Leader: Spirit of the Land,
People: help us remember our hidden history.
Leader: Suffering God,
People: help our tears to flow for the pain of the past.
Leader: Reconciling Spirit,
People: heal our shame and our wounds.

Site six: the last post

Background
During 1928 a drought in Central Australia brought the Walpiri and Aranda in conflict with the pastoralists. Water was scarce and bush tucker was hard to find. Cattle-killing increased as hunger grew. Rumours of black vengeance were rife and the manager of Coniston station called for police protection. When a local dingo trapper was killed and mutilated for refusing to return an Aboriginal woman, the local community called for vengeance to 'teach the blacks a lesson'.

The police reprisal expedition was led by a Gallipoli veteran and a tough bushman, Mounted Constable George Murray. He left Coniston Station with eight horsemen armed with guns on 16 August and returned to a hero's welcome in Alice Springs on 1 September. As many as seventy Aborigines may have been slaughtered on the expedition. The Coniston massacre is generally considered the last official massacre of Aboriginal people in Australia and illustrates the fierce racism rampant in Central Australia. According to the

Northern Territory Times, many settlers 'preferred a dead black to a live one' (Reynolds 1998, p. 195).

Story six
(Two flags, one Australian, the other Aboriginal, are located before the participants. A bugler stands at attention beneath the Australian flag. Aboriginal women are seated beneath the Aboriginal flag.)
Elder:
A veteran soldier led the raid,
remembering another war,
tall and tragic days at Gallipoli
where mates had sacrificed their lives
for their country.
Now across the same burnt country,
deep into its centre, its soul,
parched with drought,
the reprisal party rode.
They found the families in their camps,
guilty in the soldier's eyes.
They charged
and mowed them down:
twenty, thirty, seventy — maybe more.
The last war!
A few were taken prisoner and led away.
Later, unchained
one by one,
they were told to run
and shot for fun.
The red centre blazed even redder that day,
crying to God for justice,
crying to the Spirit of the Land
for the lives sacrificed in the sand.
At the going down of the sun,
and in the morning,
we will remember them.

Word six: 'Today you will be with me in paradise.'
Reader: Luke 23:39–43

Response
(To be spoken slowly with a pause between each voice.)
Voice 1: Today you will be with me in paradise.
Voice 2: Today you will be with me on an expedition.
Voice 1: Today you will be with me in paradise.
Voice 2: Today you will be with me at Gallipoli.
Voice 1: Today you will be with me in paradise.
Voice 2: Today you will be leading a charge into their camp.
Voice 1: Today you will be with me in paradise.
Voice 2: These savages are guilty.
Voice 1: This man has done nothing wrong.
Voice 2: They all deserve to die for killing a white man.
Voice 1: This man has done nothing wrong.
Voice 2: They are better off dead anyway.
Voice 1: This man has done nothing wrong.

Rite six: the last post
(The soldier plays The Last Post on the bugle to remember all who died in wars abroad. The Aboriginal women wail to remember all indigenous people who died for this land in the wars at home. A minute's silence follows.)
Leader: We blow the bugle today
People: to remember the last charge against an Aboriginal camp.
Leader: We play the last post today
People: to remember those whose lives were sacrificed unjustly.
Leader: We maintain a minute's silence
People: to hear the cries of Aboriginal ancestors
and the Spirit of the Land crying in the centre.
Leader: At the going down of the sun, and in the morning,
People: we will remember them.

Closure
Leader: Spirit of the Land,
People: help us remember our hidden history.
Leader: Suffering God,
People: help our tears to flow for the pain of the past.
Leader: Reconciling Spirit,
People: heal our shame and our wounds.

Site seven: Fountain of Tears

Background
On 31 March 1998 a striking stone monument was dedicated at the site of the former Colebrook Home where stolen Aboriginal children were institutionalised until 1971. The tragic story of how Aboriginal children were forcibly removed — 'stolen' — from their parents and placed in public institutions or private homes is recorded in *Bringing Them Home*. This report was released in 1997 and records the painful experiences of Aboriginal and Torres Strait Islander people subjected to a misguided government policy of racial assimilation. The stone monument dedicated on that Sunday in 1998 is entitled 'Fountain of Tears' and symbolises in a dramatic way the sorrow of the Aboriginal parents who lost their children. The water from the fountain flows down, from a coolamon, over the faces of six Aboriginal people into a pool of tears below. The water from that pool was used in a healing ritual for those present at the dedication of the fountain.

Story seven
(The participants gather round a fountain, a pool or a stream representing the tears of the stolen generation and all deprived Aboriginal people.)
Elder:
As we travel across this land,

searching for our soul,
we hear wailing,
deep-down wailing.
The policemen came unannounced,
they said,
and we had no time to hide
our little girl,
no time to say goodbye.
They tore her from my breast!
They tore my breast!
They tore my soul!
She screamed and screamed
as they took her off
down the long dirt track
to a 'white' prison somewhere.
In that prison,
night after night the voices of torn parents
seeped into their memories
to comfort the stolen children —
but they could not.
Day after day
the voices of their teachers crushed their hopes.
'You can be white, like us!
You can be white!'
The tears flowed
and the years flowed
until a nation heard the stolen story
and tears of healing began to flow
over many white faces.
The tears still flow
over the black faces on the monument
where Colebrook Home once stood
and kept Aboriginal 'orphans' apart,
'safe' from their culture.

Word seven: 'Woman, behold your child.'
Reader: John 19:25–27

Response
(To be spoken slowly with a pause between each voice.)
Voice 1: Woman, behold your child.
Voice 2: Woman, we're taking your son.
Voice 1: Woman, behold your child.
Voice 1: Woman we're taking your daughter.
Voice 1: Woman, behold your child.
Voice 2: Woman your child is a half-caste.
Voice 1: Woman, behold your child.
Voice 2: Woman, we are taking your child to a good home
and we will say:
Voice 1: Woman, behold your child.
Voice 2: We are doing what is best for your child.
Voice 1: Woman, behold your child.
Voice 2: We'll make your child a good Christian.
Voice 1: Woman, behold your child.
Voice 2: We're taking your child.
Voice 1: Woman, behold your child.

Rite seven: healing tears
*(Each participant dips a hand into the water and runs the
hand over the eyes of a person near by with the words, 'the
tears of a stolen child'.)*
Leader: These are the tears of the stolen generation.
People: May they help to heal our memories.
Leader: These are the tears of indigenous Australians
who suffered and died for this land.
People: May they help to heal our shame and sorrow.
Leader: These are the tears of God,
who still suffers for and with this land.
People: May they heal our broken hearts,
our broken people and our broken land.

Closure

Leader: Spirit of the Land,
People: help us remember our hidden history.
Leader: Suffering God,
People: help our tears to flow for the pain of the past.
Leader: Reconciling Spirit,
People: heal our shame and our wounds.

BIBLIOGRAPHY

Albrecht, P. 1998, 'Aboriginal Identity and Native Title', *News Weekly*,
   7 March, pp. 11–14.
ATSIC (Aboriginal and Torres Strait Islander Commission) 1998, *As a
   Matter of Fact. Answering the Myths and Misconceptions about
   Indigenous Australians*, Office of Public Affairs, Canberra.
Baxter, J. K. 1971, *Jerusalem Daybook*, Price Milburn, Wellington.
Bird, C. 1998, *The Stolen Children, Their Stories*, Random House,
   Sydney.
Brady, V. 1998, 'Rainbow Spirit Theology: An Extended Review',
   Interface, 1, pp. 84–91.
Brennan, F. (ed.) 1994, *Reconciling Our Differences. A Christian
   Approach to Recognising Aboriginal Land Rights*, David Lovell,
   Richmond.
Bringing Them Home: see *National Inquiry into the Separation of
   Aboriginal and Torres Strait Islander Children from their Parents*,
   1997.
Brown, M. 1998a, 'The Business of Reconciliation', *For a Change*, 11,
   1, pp. 14–15.
Brown, M. 1998b, 'A Nation in Search of Its Soul', *For A Change*, 11,
   1, pp. 113–16.
Byrne, B. 1992, 'Homecoming: Scriptural Reflections upon a Process of
   Reconciliation', in *Reconciling Our Differences*, ed. F. Brennan,
   Aurora, Richmond, pp. 78–92.
Clark, M. 1976, *A Discovery of Australia*, 1976 Boyer Lectures, The
   Australian Broadcasting Commission, London.
Cone, J. 1997, *God of the Oppressed*, rev. edn, Orbis, Maryknoll.

Council for Aboriginal Reconciliation 1993a, *Making Things Right*, Commonwealth Government Publishing Service, Canberra.

—— 1993b, *Australians for Reconciliation Study Circle Kit*, Commonwealth Government Publishing Service, Canberra.

—— 1994a, *Walking Together: The First Steps*, Commonwealth Government Publishing Service, Canberra.

—— 1994b, *Valuing Cultures*, Commonwealth Government Publishing Service, Canberra.

—— 1995, *Going Forward. Social Justice for the First Australians*, Commonwealth Government Publishing Service, Canberra.

—— 1997a, *Overview. Proceedings of the Reconciliation Convention*, Book 1, Commonwealth Government Printer, Canberra.

—— 1997b, *Community. Reconciliation in the Community*, Book 2, Commonwealth Government Printer, Canberra.

—— 1997c, *Human Rights. Human Rights and Indigenous Australians*, Book 3, Commonwealth Government Printer, Canberra.

Crotty et al. 1991, *Finding a Way: Religious Worlds of Today*, HarperCollins, Melbourne.

Davis, J. 1992, *Black Life: Poems*, Queensland University Press, St Lucia.

Delphin-Stanford, D. & Brown, J. 1994, *Committed to Change: Covenanting in the Uniting Church*, The Uniting Church Press, Melbourne.

Dodson, M. 1997, 'Land Rights and Social Justice', in *Our Land Is Our Life*, ed. G. Yunupingu, Queensland University Press, St Lucia, pp. 39–51.

Dodson, P. 1993, *In Recognition: The Way Forward*, Australian Council for Social Justice, Melbourne.

—— 1996, *Reconciliation at the Crossroads*, Australian Government Publishing Service, Canberra.

Duroux, M. 1992, *Dirge for Hidden Art*, Heritage Publishing, Moruya.

Edwards, D. 1988, 'Sin and Salvation in the Southland of the Holy Spirit', in *Discovering an Australian Theology*, ed. P. Malone, St Pauls, Homebush, pp. 89–102.

Eze, E. C. (ed.) 1997, *Race and the Enlightenment: A Reader*, Blackwell, London.

Foucault, M. 1980, *Power/Knowledge: Selected Interviews and Other Writings*, ed. C. Gordon, Pantheon, New York.

Gaita, R. 1998, 'Justice, Guilt and Shame: Mapping the Conceptual Geography of Reconciliation', *Interface*, 1, pp. 5–19.

Gilbert, K. 1996, 'God at the Campfire and That Christ Fella', in *Aboriginal Spirituality, Past, Present and Future*, ed. A. Pattel-Gray, HarperCollins, Melbourne, pp. 54–65.

Gloyne, J. & Wilson, B. 1992, *The Slip-rails are Down. An Anthology of Country Poems*, Kookaburra Press, Adelaide.

Gondarra, D. 1988, *Father You Gave Us the Dreaming*, Nungalinya College, Darwin.

—— 1998, '*Madayin* — A System of Law and Governance', annual Adelaide College of Divinity lecture, Adelaide.

Grassby, A. & Hill, M. 1988, *Six Australian Battlefields*, Allen & Unwin, Sydney.

Habel, N. 1985, *The Book of Job*, Westminster, Philadelphia.

—— 1992, 'The Suffering Land Ideology in Jeremiah', *Lutheran Theological Journal*, 26, pp. 14–26.

—— 1995, *The Land is Mine. Six Biblical Land Ideologies*, Fortress, Minneapolis.

—— 1996, 'The Crucified Land: Towards Our Reconciliation with the Earth', *Colloquium*, 28, 2, pp. 3–18.

—— 1998a, 'The Reconciliation Process in Australia: A Challenge for the Churches', *Interface*, 1, pp. 53–65.

Hamilton, A. 1998, 'In Whose Name? Reconciliation, Responsibility and the Churches', *Interface*, 1, pp. 43–52.

Hanson, P. 1998, speech on The UN Draft Declaration on the Rights of Indigenous Peoples, 2 June [Online, accessed 4 Nov. 1998]. URL: http://www.gwb.com.au/onenation/speeches/landttle.html

Harris, C. 1996, 'Guidelines for So-Called Western Civilisation and Western Christianity', in *Aboriginal Spirituality*, ed. A. Pattel-Gray, HarperCollins, Melbourne, pp. 66–78.

Harris, J. 1990, *One Blood. 200 Years of Aboriginal Encounter with Christianity: A Story of Hope*, Albatross, Sutherland.

Henderson, M. 1996, *The Forgiveness Factor. Stories of Hope in a World of Conflict*, Grosvenor, London.

Hollinsworth, D. 1998, *Race and Racism in Australia*, 2nd edn, Social Science Press, Katoomba.

Holst, W. 1996, 'After the Apologies: Discerning and Applying Native Spiritual Traditions in the Canadian Churches', *Mission*, 3, 2, pp. 153–61.

Horton, D. (ed.) 1994, *Encyclopedia of Aboriginal Australia*, vol. 2, Aboriginal Studies Press, Canberra.

Howard, G. 1995, 'Unravelling Racism: Reflections on the Role of Non-Indigenous People — Supporting Indigenous Education', *Australasian Engineering Journal*, 6, 2, pp. 122–8.

Kelly, T. 1990, *A New Imagining. Towards an Australian Spirituality*, Collins Dove, Melbourne.

Knight, D. 1956, *Poetical Works of Henry Lawson*, Angus & Robertson, Sydney.

Lilburne, G. 1989, *A Sense of Place. A Christian Theology of the Land*, Abingdon, Nashville.

Loubser, J. A. 1987, *The Apartheid Bible: A Critical Review of Racial Theology in South Africa*, Maskew Miller Longman, Cape Town.

Lutheran Hymnal 1973, Lutheran Publishing House, Adelaide.

McConnochie, K., Hollinsworth, D. & Pettman, J. 1989, *Race and Racism in Australia*, Social Science Press, Wentworth Falls.

McQueen, H. 1970, *A New Britannia*, Penguin, Sydney.

Manning, K. 1998, 'We Are Truly Sorry', *Social Justice Trends*, 89, p. 4.

Martin, R. 1980, 'Reconciliation and Forgiveness in the Letter to the Colossians', in *Reconciliation and Hope*, ed. R. Banks, Paternoster Press, Exeter.

Mattingley, C. 1988, *Survival in Our Own Land. 'Aboriginal' Experiences in South Australia Since 1836*, Hodder & Stoughton, Sydney.

Moltmann, J. 1974, *The Crucified God*, SCM, London.

Moore, B. 1992, *Racism: A History of Ideas*, unpublished paper, University of South Australia, Adelaide.

—— 1993, 'Anti-Racist Education: South Australian Policy in Black Perspective', in *South Australian Educational Leader*, 4, 1, pp. 1–11.

Mudrooroo 1995, *Us Mob. History, Culture Struggle: An Introduction to Indigenous Australia*, Angus & Robertson, Sydney.

Mueller-Fahrenholz, G. 1997, *The Art of Forgiveness. Theological Reflections on Healing and Reconciliation*, WCC Productions, Geneva.

Myers, F. 1986, *Pintubi Country. Pintubi Self*, Australian Institute of Aboriginal Studies, Canberra.

National Inquiry into the Separation of Aboriginal and Torres Strait Islander Children from Their Parents 1997, *Bringing Them Home*, ed. R. Wilson, Human Rights and Equal Opportunity Commission, Sydney.

National Report 1991: see Royal Commission into Aboriginal Deaths in Custody, 1991.

Pattel-Gray, A. 1996, *Aboriginal Spirituality, Past, Present and Future*, HarperCollins, Melbourne.

—— 1998, *The Great White Flood. Racism in Australia*, Scholars Press, Atlanta.

Pattel-Gray, A. & Brown, J. P. 1997, *Indigenous Australia. A Dialogue about the Word Becoming Flesh in Aboriginal Cultures*, WCC Publications, Geneva.

Pearson, N. 1997, 'The Concept of Native Title at Common Law', in *Our Land Is Our Life: Land Rights — Past, Present and Future*, ed. G. Yunupingu, Queensland University Press, St Lucia, pp. 150–162.

Pickard, S. 1998, 'The View from the Verandah: Gospel and Spirituality in an Australian Setting', unpublished paper, ANZSTS conference.

Poland, W. G. F. 1988, *Loose Leaves. Reminiscences of a Pioneer North Queensland Missionary*, Lutheran Publishing House, Adelaide.

Pryor, B. 1998, *Maybe Tomorrow*, Penguin, Sydney.

Rainbow Spirit Elders 1997, *Rainbow Spirit Theology: Towards an Australian Aboriginal Theology*, HarperCollins, Melbourne.

Reed-Gilbert, K. 1997, *Message Stick. Contemporary Aboriginal Writing*, Jukurrpa Books, Adelaide.

Reynolds, H. 1989, *Dispossession. Black Australians and White Invaders*, Allen & Unwin, Sydney.

—— 1992, *The Law of the Land*, 2nd edn, Penguin, Melbourne.

—— 1996, *Frontier. Reports from the Edge of White Settlement*, Allen & Unwin, Sydney.

—— 1998, *This Whispering in Our Hearts*, Allen & Unwin, Sydney.

Ridgeway, A. 1997, 'Rights of the First Dispossessed: The New South Wales Situation', in *Our Land Is Our Life*, ed. G. Yunupingu, Queensland University Press, St Lucia, pp. 63–79.

Rintoul, S. 1993, *The Wailing. A National Black Oral History*, Heinemann, Melbourne.

Rose, D. 1992, *Dingo Makes Us Human. Life and Land in an Australian Aboriginal Culture*, Cambridge University Press, Cambridge.

—— 1991, *Hidden Histories*, Aboriginal Studies Press, Canberra.

Rowley, C. 1970, *The Destruction of Aboriginal Society*, ANU Press, Canberra.

Royal Commission into Aboriginal Deaths in Custody 1991, *National Report: Overview and Recommendations*, Australian Government Publishing Service, Canberra.

Royal Commission into British Nuclear Tests in Australia 1985, *Report*, Australian Government Publishing Service, Canberra.

Schmiechen, P. 1996, *Christ the Reconciler: A Theology for Opposites, Differences and Enemies*, Eerdmans, Grand Rapids.

Schnackenburg, R. 1990, *Ephesians. A Commentary*, T & T Clark, Edinburgh.

Soelle, D. 1975, *Suffering*, Fortress, Philadelphia.

—— 1995, *Theology for Skeptics, Reflections on God*, Fortress, Minneapolis.

Stepan, N. 1982, *The Idea of Race in Science*, Archon, Hamden, Conn.

Stockton, E. 1995, *The Aboriginal Gift. Spirituality for a Nation*, Millennium Books, Sydney.

Strehlow, T. G. H. 1971, *Songs of Central Australia*, Angus & Robertson, Sydney.

—— 1977, 'Religious Beliefs of the Australian Aborigine', *Forum 69*, Jan., pp. 4–17.

Strelan, J. 1989, '*Theologia Crucis, Theologia Gloriae*. A Study in Opposing Theologies', *Lutheran Theological Journal*, 23, pp. 99–113.

Swain, T. 1993, *A Place for Strangers*, Cambridge University Press, Cambridge.

Tacey, D. 1995, *Edge of the Sacred. Transformation in Australia*, HarperCollins, Melbourne.

Tatz, C & McConnochie, K. 1975, *Black Viewpoints*, ANZ Book Co., Sydney.

Victorin-Vangerud, N. 1997, 'The Spirit's Struggle: Reconciliation in Moltmann's *pneumatologia crucis*', *Colloquium*, 29, pp. 95–103.

Villa-Vincencio, C. 1997, 'Telling One Another Stories', in *The Reconciliation of All Peoples*, ed. G. Baum & H. Wells, Orbis, Maryknoll.

Volf, M. 1996, *Exclusion and Embrace: A Theological Exploration of Identity, Otherness and Reconciliation*, Abingdon, Nashville.

Wilson, R. 1997: see National Inquiry into the Separation of Aboriginal and Torres Strait Islander Children from their Families 1997.

Wink, W. 1998, *When Powers Fall. Reconciliation in the Healing of Nations*, Fortress, Minneapolis.

Yunupingu, G. 1996, 'Concepts of Land and Spirituality', in *Aboriginal Spirituality, Past, Present and Future*, ed. A. Pattel-Gray, HarperCollins, Melbourne, pp. 4–10.

—— (ed.) 1997, *Our Land Is Our Life. Land Rights — Past, Present and Future*, Queensland University Press, St Lucia.

INDEX